True Tall Tales

By

Vondas A. Smith

Edited by RaNae Smith Vaughn

ISBN: 1-4033-8248-4(softcover)
ISBN: 1-4033-8247-6(electronic)
ISBN: 1-4033-8249-2(dustcover)

Library of Congress Control Number: 2002094962

This book is printed on acid free paper.

Printed in the United States of America
Bloomington, IN

1st Books - rev. 10/24/02

Preface

This collection of stories is true, first-hand accounts of events during the author's life. Names of places and dates are accurate. Many individuals' names, however, have been changed to protect identities.

July 31, 2003

There is no fear that a man should fear more, than the fear that he doesn't fear God enough.

Contents

Chapter 7—Learning From Others

Chapter 8—The Home, Workplace

Chapter 9—Living Abroad

Chapter 10—Away From Home

Soldier Buddy's Secret

Written September 23, 1989

Two 18-year-old soldiers met during their basic training in southwest Missouri's Camp Crowder before the atomic bomb ended World War II. The elder by a few months was Ruben, a Yankee from Indianapolis. The quieter of the two was drafted from northeast Arkansas within days of finishing his 11th grade of high school. The war was over in Europe and these two, soon-to-be pals, shared a common lot with all the other smooth-faced recruits. A much scared and decorated Corporal named Jonas did not stutter when he told them why they were there on the first day of their Army basic training. That vet from the battles of Europe had seen enough blood and guts to know what war was, and his first words to all of them were unforgettable. "Men, you're here to learn how to kill and how to keep from being killed," Corporal Jonas spoke loudly.

It had been fully 3 ½ years since Pearl Harbor, and the wartime mobilization and change had denied the average boy a normal adolescent life. In those days, boys seemed to become men before their time. Ruben was already married at 18. His buddy, Sadnov, was engaged but would be jilted before basic training was over. It was a terribly hot summer, and the training was sobering and tough. German prisoners of war, generally older men, performed much of the menial work about the camp. All of the newly drafted foot soldiers silently knew that after training they were headed to the South Pacific.

At the end of an especially full day of hard training, being physically exhausted, the sober-minded youths were all present and accounted for in their bunks—asleep. At some unknown hour of the night, Sadnov's bed seemed to come apart with a hard jolt, throwing him head first to the floor.

His sleep was over. He wasn't one to panic easily, so he continued to lie there with feet and legs tilted high in the air. Even in the dark, it was clear what had happened.

The head of the bed had collapsed, bringing his head and shoulders to the floor. Quickly enough, he was aware that he wasn't injured, but his position was uncomfortable enough for him to want to do something about his predicament—immediately. Being suspicious that someone had planned the bed's collapse, he listened in the stillness for a giggle from some prankster soldier. However, there wasn't a peep in the night's silence. Pretending to still be asleep, Sadnov passed some time in that position, but this brought him more misery with the passing minutes. Finally, he quietly got up to put his bed back together. It appeared that not one single fellow had awakened in the barracks, except Sadnov.

For the soldier in training, there was a ten-minute rest period in every hour of his workday. On the following day, during one of these short periods, the two buddies engaged in some small talk. First off, Ruben was sworn to absolute secrecy. He promised that as a true pal he would tell no one. Only then did Sadnov, still angry for having fallen victim to someone's childish prank, tell his true bosom army buddy about his harrowing night.

In their wartime world, there was no place for pranksters or time for play. Neither of them had a smile, just plain disgust and disdain for such foolishness. They promised each other that the clown that did such a thing would never have the satisfaction of learning that he succeeded. From that, they went back to their work, learning from Corporal Jonas and others how to win the war.

About a week later, the two buddies were sharing in one of their frequent times together. Only this time, it was Ruben that seemed to be the troubled one. He wanted to seriously share something of great importance, but he didn't want Sadnov to be angry nor troubled about it. After being very careful to make sure that Sadnov would keep it in absolute confidence, Ruben lowered his voice and began. "As a real pal, do you promise not to tell anyone?" His reply from a true buddy was, "Never, never." "And you won't be angry when I tell you?" asked Ruben. "Not in the least," replied Sadnov. That was when Ruben relaxed and said, "I'm the one that fixed your bed to fall the other night."

Epilogue: After training, Ruben was sent to Europe in the U.S. occupational forces. He was wounded in a battle with holdout enemy forces. After having a minor part in the Nuremberg trials, he returned to the U.S. to find that his marriage had fallen apart. After more than 42 years, the two soldier buddies coincidentally met again. Ruben was employed in Alaska in U.S. defense and was on vacation in the south. Sadnov had been a resident in South America for many years, and he was also vacationing in the U.S.

Vondas A. Smith

Just Don't Worry About It

Written September 26, 1989

As surely as there are so many, many people—and each is identified by a different name—there must also be as many varying degrees of conscientiousness about being "our brother's keeper." Of course, a man's judgment is not final, but it certainly isn't anathema to be a commentator speaking about his own observations. If it were forbidden to comment concerning information he was privy to, how else could one ever become a witness? This divulgence certainly isn't intended to be judgmental; however, it can serve to substantiate a point of contention.

At the close of World War II, there were literally millions of men and women in uniform. Some of these, hyperbolically speaking, had earned more medals; battle ribbons, and stars, than they had clothes to pin them on. The camps in the continental U.S. were overflowing with battle-worn and weary soldiers awaiting discharge. Even former prisoner-of-war camps, formerly occupied by German and Japanese prisoners of war, served as temporary housing for the returned soldiers from overseas. There was little more for this multitude to do except eat, sleep, and wait their time for discharge. It wasn't uncommon for old acquaintances to meet again. It was such an occasion of getting together again that sets the scene of this recount.

There were four soldiers, two of whom were long-time, close friends even before being in uniform. These were drawn together in an army camp that was functioning as a discharge center for veterans. One of the four soldiers owned a fine automobile. This was a mark of status during those times when, for three years, no automobiles were made for the buying public. The common bond that welded the four together was their Christian

4

faith. They were always looking for some special church activity or function to attend.

Several hours away, in another state, there was a bible school that was placed on their visiting agenda. They pooled the expense money for the automobile trip, chose a weekend, and were off. It was a most enjoyable visit, uplifting, and they decided to make a return trip in due time.

To identify at least one of these by name, he will be called J or Jay. The J was adopted from Junior, and he truly was one that carried his dad's given name. He only had one given name when he entered the army, and for record purposes, he had to adopt another; therefore, he borrowed the J from Junior. Jay had earned a stripe or two due to his status as a combat veteran and for the length of his service. With his rank of promotion, he found himself serving as the mail clerk of his holding company. This job obligation was just a little confining to him, whereas his long-time buddy didn't have any job duties.

Another weekend was decided upon for their return visit to the bible school. When Jay's closest buddy was told to get his quota of cash together for the upcoming weekend, he bluntly replied that there was no way. "There is no way whatsoever that I will be able to make this trip," Jay heard from his friend. Of course, just to say that there is "no way" doesn't explain anything. Close friends learn, out of respect for each other, to do some confiding. Jay proposed a loan if it were a matter of being short on cash. Jay thought that he had eliminated every argument his friend had made, but the decision remained that his friend wasn't going. "You've got to tell me why you can't go," demanded Jay. "You write your own liberty pass, the money won't be a problem, and you surely want to go, so why won't you go?"

Jay's buddy held out, keeping his reason to himself almost longer than Jay's patience cared to endure. After much insistence by Jay, the agitated friend saw that his guarded secret would have to be surrendered in the interest of peace. "All right, I'll tell you why I'm not going, but it won't change anything in the least, because I'm still not going," said his friend. "I have no intention of going to that bible school and staying in their visitors' quarters, because I've caught a bad case of the itch, and I am not going to take it to that bible school." Jay was jubilant to hear such a trivial argument. "Don't worry about it! That's no reason for you not to go," he insisted. "I've had it for weeks!"

Epilogue: Jay earned his battle stars in the European Theater of War in 1944. He and his three friends all became ministers. After his military service, Jay married and became a pastor in Birmingham, Alabama. His friend founded two churches in the U.S., and subsequently, he served 24 years as a foreign missionary. The author and Jay remained remotely associated throughout life until Jay's death on or about December 8, 2000.

She, Yolanda, Married Me

Written November 16, 1989, Bolivia, South America

Prologue: Three men exchanged greetings while attending a church conference in Tulsa, Oklahoma, on an October afternoon in 1967. They were long-time acquaintances, but nearly two decades had passed since they had seen each other. Two of these were single men when they first knew one another, but they had long since married. They had plenty to talk about to fill in those years of time. During a time of evangelistic activity, while yet an unmarried youth, one of the ministers had met a young lady whose name was Yolanda. Spanish was her native language, and not once was there a conversation between the young preacher and Yolanda. He didn't speak Spanish, and she knew no English.

Yolanda followed their evangelistic group for nearly a week during a series of one-night meetings in Mexico. Each night, she would be sitting near the front, dressed in white. She was a secretary by profession, and her note pad and pencil were as much a part of her as her lovely olive complexion. Those impressions of Yolanda were lasting.

It was Ardell, while a young preacher, who had formed the vivid memory of Yolanda. As the three men chatted in Tulsa that afternoon after their greetings, handshakes, and smiles, their talk was about old times down in Mexico. All the knowledgeable topics and things in common had entered conversation and been spent. With little left to them to talk about, Ardell posed a question. It was directed to the older of his friends, whose name was Maclovio. "Did you ever know a young secretary named Yolanda?" asked Ardell. With the question, he proceeded to explain as much as he could remember about the impressionable young lady.

During those years in question, Maclovio was the director of a Bible Institute in Mexico City. Such a question from Ardell to him wasn't completely an unreasonable one. She could have possibly been or become a student of the school at some time. Maclovio began to search his memory while Isidro, who had the least to talk about, came up with the answer. "I know her," he responded. "She married me."

The subject died more quickly than it was introduced. Ardell didn't dare say that he had named a daughter after Isidro's wife.

Alvie, Super Survivor

Written October 10, 1989

All creatures of our great, earth community don't have the troubling complexes and peer pressure hang-ups of humans. There was once a lovely creature of the feline species that was known to his friends and admirers as Alvie. Destiny for Alvie grew out of his own choices. He chose the house that he planned to call home, and he adopted the family that lived there as his supporters. And since there were three children in the home, he had some ready-made friends.

Alvie may have been intelligent as a cat, but he wasn't very wise. He developed the warm habit of sleeping on the car motor at night during his first winter. Unquestionably, he had a good lifestyle. In his new surroundings, it was not important that he was once scathingly looked upon as an alley cat.

On one frosty morning, as the madam of the house was about to leave for work, she cranked the car. Suddenly Alvie came tearing from beneath the car in a fast getaway. The fast cat successfully performed his acrobatics for a few mornings. However, his sleeping quarters on top of the car motor ultimately brought him a whack in the back one morning as he was making his fast exit. He finally became a *first-time loser* in making his usual clean getaway. He survived what was thought to be a blow from the rotating fan of the car motor.

Dear Alvie was gentle enough to have gained the admiration of the three children in the home. He got more than casual attention, for they saw that he didn't have to forage far from home for something to eat. The madam of the house, and mother of the three children, knew well of the mutual attraction between the feline and the admiring children.

Unfortunately, the love affair between the cat and children brought great consternation to the mother on one particularly cold morning. As usual, she cranked the car without a thought of Alvie, and on that morning, Alvie wasn't thinking either. From beneath the hood of the car, there came the unmistakable thundering of great repairs in progress or great destruction taking place. Then came a catcall for help, but it was short lived.

No one having heard what took place needed to be informed that the carnage would be horrifying. That mother of three children had no intention whatsoever to put her hand to the gruesome task of removing cat fur and flesh from the car motor, and doubly so at home where the children were sure to learn of the fate of their feline friend. She pointed the car in the direction of a neighborhood car service center and made her first stop for the day. Little explanation was necessary as the helpful hand of a service attendant removed the bloodied carcass and placed its near lifeless form in a cardboard box. A little life in the creature seemed apparent, but it was not enough to allow the cat to attempt a getaway. Poor Alvie had become a *second-time loser.*

The second stop for the day had to be at the veterinarian's office. The distraught mother with a dying cat wouldn't know how to tell her children about the fate of dear Alvie. Possibly she didn't talk with absolute coherence when she instructed the veterinarian to dispose of him. Be it that, or a code of ethics that he must abide by, or perhaps it was the challenge to preserve life, who knows why the vet decided to start sewing up Alvie?

At home later, the mother broke the news to three children who mourned the passing of their pet. The statement from the vet would come later for having disposed of it, but that would be the easier part.

Surprisingly, a few days later a phone call came from the vet's office. He politely informed a member of the family that they could drop by at anytime and pick up their pet. It was a surprise to all, but to the children it was a most pleasant one. To avoid the growing cost of hospitalization and kennel keep, one of the parents went by to pick up the not-so-wanted cat. Lovingly, he was received back into the familiar arms of children, but he seemed only a part of his former self.

Part of an ear was gone, and something had made a clean cut to dispose of his tail. Skin, once peeled away to lay bare his bloodied carcass, had been neatly trimmed and sewed back into place. Scars told part of the story. He moved slowly with a limp that belied the fact that he did not escape fractures. Both testicles were forever gone which would deny him parenthood in anyone's alley. Alvie was ruined, and anyone on earth except that one vet would have known it.

He was a great survivor—that Alvie—and the admiration and attention that he got from the children seemed to exceed any that he got before. The parents were genuinely delighted and pleased to find the children so happy once again. It wasn't important that Alvie's pedigree didn't have show animal and prize-winning qualities. The children were happy, and nothing else seemed to be important.

On the first of the month, the great bill collector makes his entry into every home by way of the U.S. mail system. It was then shockingly learned that, bedsides making children happy, Alvie had some other capabilities. The dutiful collector was asking for more that $400 for the gentle care received at the veterinarian hospital.

The unhappy parents examined the statement of charges and tried to give it place in the family budget. As the fretful mother and father pondered the mounting disadvantages of being adopted by the super-survivor feline, Alvie became a *third-time loser*. He lost his pettishly called name, Alvie, to become the lowly D.C. To the parents, D.C. was an abbreviation that didn't stand for Darling Cat.

Harmony In One Word

Written November 10, 1989, Bolivia, South America

<u>Prologue</u>: The woman mentioned here did not enjoy a long lifespan, but a voluminous record would have to be written to recount her loveliness as a Christian, a wife, and mother of children. Born a citizen of North America, she was still a new bride when she found herself making her new home in India with her missionary husband. His church labors abroad brought them frequent separations due to his travels. During those years, she developed a strength and resolve that is not common to women. This ability that she possessed, to stand with a decisive and confident posture, never needed to be told. Her strength stood evident, yet she was warm and vibrant. No one ever had cause to feel uncomfortable when she was present.

The story about to be told may have a humorous note if one wished to have it that way. It took place on a ski slope high in the Andean Mountains. The air was terribly thin, and those that are born and live out their lives in that locale have a 20 percent greater lung capacity than those at sea level.

She was Audry, and the husband we call Hugh. The host, Ardell, had a small party of four that included them. These two had seen more of the planet earth than most people would ever dream of seeing. Even with their extensive traveling, Hugh admitted that he had never had his feet on the ground at such a high altitude. The official height was 17,318 feet above sea level.

Hugh appeared to be ready for any reasonable challenge. He had conquered a new height on the planet earth; but he wasn't alone. With feet well planted in the snow, his dear wife, Audry, was near him. The scenery around them was stupendous. They looked out into space at snow-covered peaks of the Andean Mountains for scores of miles. Near at hand was one last slope that was easily accessible from where they stood. It was perhaps another 300 feet higher.

The mountain is named Chacalataya, and skiers from all over the world go to that mountain just to be able to say they've conquered the highest ski slope. Indeed, some have died in their efforts. The point where Hugh and Audry stood that afternoon served as a parking lot for jeeps and other vehicles. With alertness, Audry overheard the casual suggestion from the guide as he suggested that Hugh accompany him to the last peak. At that point, nothing would obscure their vision out over the world.

There can't be found such a woman as Audry who stood in such a delicate physical frame, pale-faced for need of oxygen, but alert to the occasion. That dear little wife pronounced one word with a sure tone of voice. She didn't argue, command, nor show a bad attitude. Neither was she excited or frightened. She simply said, "Hugh." Their guide still smiles today when he thinks of it. Such harmonious understanding between husband and wife has never been greater than that which those two displayed that afternoon. While Audry's feet were well planted in the frozen snow, and her lungs labored for every molecule of oxygen, she was resolved to protect their common interest by seeing that he didn't further jeopardize a bad situation.

Epilogue: Hugh and his guide glanced at one another without a word. Each knew fully well that the woman's discernment for the hour's need had just dictated the solution. Great understanding and final decision came when she simply pronounced her husband's name.

~~~~~~~~~~~~~~~~~~~~~~~~~~~~~~~~~~~~~

Foul Taste In the Dark

Written September 23, 1989

During those growing teen years, Sadnov was a pimple-faced youth that brought most of his acne trouble upon himself. There was one particular summer that he ate, almost single-handily, everything sweet that his mother had canned. She was a country mother and knew how to can fruits, vegetables, and jellies, and she always did a lot of it for her family. Sadnov was scolded when his mother realized that her reserve of preserves and jellies were growing short. His sweet tooth always called for more until there was no more to be enjoyed, and he finally came to be without his mother's jelly canning. Sadnov especially liked it with bread, but that wasn't absolutely necessary. It could come straight from the jar in a heaping spoon full.

Somewhere within days before the great jelly famine truly befell them all, a tired and sweaty bare-shouldered boy ran madly into the house for his sweet tooth "fix." It was beginning to grow a little dark at the end of the day. He had no sooner gotten his hand on the spoon before he hastily reached up to the cupboard above his head for his succulent treat. There was the jar, and it was full, even had the cap still on it. Like magic it was uncapped, and as quickly as lightening, a heaping spoonful was placed in his mouth. There it was, but then it wasn't.

Somewhere between those two seconds, in a time space too short to measure, Sadnov spat out the jelly. The place for the jar in the cupboard was right, the jar size was correct, in the dark the color didn't matter, who bothers to smell it, and it truly was jelly. But never before had the master jelly taster savored such and called it fruit jelly. He replaced the cap, cleaned up his mess somewhat, and put his taste for jelly on hold for the present.

A short while later his curiosity to know what happened carried him back. The light was switched on this time, and a label was clearly seen on the jar. Someone had purchased a cleaning agent of beautiful savory color, in jell form, and put it high in the cupboard where the homemade jellies were. When he had dashed into the kitchen a little earlier with the appetite of Esau and as weak as a bald-headed Samson, the jelly pirate had not wasted time reading labels.

That product may not even be on the market in these more modern times, but know for sure that it was a good product. For whatever purpose it was put there, and by whom, that now takes second place in importance. Sadnov gained enough jelly sense to last a lifetime. Now he knows: Read the label, and then enjoy the product.

~~~~~~~~~~~~~~~~~~~~~~~~~~~~~~~~~~~~

Getting to Know Granddad

Written October 16, 1998

In the southwest corner of Townsend Cemetery, the gravediggers struggled in the rock and stone to dig a grave deep enough to bury Granddad Al Smith. He died in 1960 at 86 years of age. His wife and a bachelor son were buried beside him later. Granddad Al was not a colorful man to know, and alcohol kept him off the community list of the most righteous. In stature he did not tower as a big man, his education was minimal, he had no trade or profession, but he did have a positive side. He married one wife, they had ten children, and most of them survived him even after about 65 years of marriage. In the town of Smithville, Arkansas, population 61, there are still country folks around that remember Al Smith. Remembering him, and they all do, is not enough for some grandchildren that understand a difference between remembering him and knowing him.

One of those grandchildren, who here will be called Grandson, was the first born to one of Al Smith's four sons. Grandson was intrigued by the frontier surroundings in the Ozark Mountains of Arkansas, and he cherished every visit to see his grandparents. Grandson lived with his parents and two brothers in a larger city about 50 miles away, but country road conditions and troublesome private transportation made visits nearly impossible most of the time. Besides the travel difficulty, there was another real obstacle. That other obstacle was big, and it came in the person of Grandson's mother. His mother knew well that when the men of the Smith family got together, in a few hours they would all be drunk on hard liquor. There were no exceptions. When Grandson's dad wished to see his parents in the mountains, the fight began in his home. The fight at home lasted until there were enough promises to fill volumes, but the books were thrown out once the crippled old Ford was cranked and headed toward Smithville.

As much as possible, Grandson's mother kept her part of the Smith clan separated from the elder Al Smith and sons. World War II had rations on gasoline and tires, and there were shortages of everything to keep an old car operating. It was a confining and hard time to live. The wartime Selective Service System took every able-bodied youth away from home, including Grandson; therefore, visits to Granddad Al were eliminated until the war was over. Also added to these restrictions were three years in college, marriage, a family of children of his own, and 23 years as a foreign resident, and it's evident that Grandson never had much more than just memories of Granddad Al or any other elders of the Smith family.

Seeing Granddad gave rare times when Grandson could write names and dates or a few choice bits of information. When Granddad Al would talk, it was verbal history to Grandson. He remembered it all and recorded much of it on bits of paper with a pencil. Granddad Al told Grandson how he could tell the difference between Jessie and Frank James before he moved from St. Joseph, Missouri, at age nine. Granddad Al said Frank carried a dog in the saddle with him, but Jessie wouldn't. Granddad told how he helped drive the cattle from St. Joseph to the mountains of Arkansas when the family moved. His mother Liza married Jim Williams and had a family but nothing was ever said about his own dad. Some things remain in question about how he met Grandmother who is said to have come from Sweetwater, Texas. She was born in 1875, and why that Pueblo girl was so far from her tribal country in New Mexico isn't known.

Aunt Mary Ann, one of Granddad Al's daughters, once told how other children in school repeatedly annoyed and irritated the Smith children by asking them what nationality they were. Mary Ann asked her dad, Granddad

Al, that question at home, and he dismissed it by saying that they were Scott-Irish. It could be that he was, but his children weren't. In turn, one of his daughters married Mike Salas, whose native language was Spanish.

Another great-granddaughter in Granddad Al's bloodline married a grandson to Russian Jewish immigrants to the U.S., while still another married a Bolivian man whose native tongue is Ketchua. One grandson, two generations removed, married a girl that grew up in South Africa and speaks Afrikaans, the language of that country. Two other Native American tribes are identified as having married into Granddad Al's great grandchildren.

In a return trip one day to the old home place in the mountains, Grandson and his wife elected to take along with them an 87-year-old widowed daughter-in-law and another grandson to Granddad Al. A telephone call was made to inform Granddad Al's granddaughter who lives in the old family house. It was then that he learned that she could not be in town that day. It was a beautiful day, however, and Grandson with another three relatives elected to go anyway. When the four arrived in the mountains, they were unaccompanied as they visited the old cemetery and the grounds of the tiny mountain home. Those retired older folks walked over the rocks and among the few trees of the old home place, mostly looking and remembering.

The voice of dear old Granddad Al had been silent for nearly four decades. Had he been at home that day he would have said, "Howdy to all of younses, come right on in. It's been a right smart good while since we hered or seen ye. Tell us about yourselves."

That widowed and quiet-mannered little woman, living alone on the old home place, is Granddad Al's granddaughter. She speaks no Spanish as her father did. She was under 10 years old when Granddad Al died leaving only some memories of Granddad whom she didn't truly know. Notwithstanding, she displayed a kindness in Granddad Al's stead that day. Had Granddad Al not have done what his lovely little granddaughter did; he surely would have smiled his approval upon her for having done it. Before leaving town that morning, Dolores Maria Salas Davis, went by the old post office café and arranged for all her four family visitors to have lunch at the best place in town.

With the other three, Grandson left the Ozarks that afternoon with a feeling in heart that he had been in the shadows of his frontier Granddad. He and Grandmother Margaret were there in the person of Dolores Maria's hospitality, and it conjured memories to make our Granddad Al to be real once again.

~~~~~~~~~~~~~~~~~~~~~~~~~~~

Finding Dad's Family

Written June 17, 2002

After more than 25 years of marriage and having a lovely daughter and two fine sons in high school and college, their wayward husband and father walked away. When financial support diminished in their abandoned family, RaNae simply extended herself into the job market for a second job. With her college degree as a librarian, there was no need for job training. She merely added a second schedule to fill the vacuum in their one-parent family.

In her new lifestyle, and being alone to support her family, RaNae and her mother instinctively reached out to one another again after so many years. They had spent more than 20 years living apart on two American continents. Her parents, racing through their seventh decade in life, had moved back to the United States in retirement. When the new century made its debut, the frequency of family events was on the increase with every season. Among grandchildren, there were high school graduations, a college graduation, and two marriages. Most of those grandchildren were nieces and nephews to RaNae. Two members of a new generation of great-grandchildren were added as the clan irrefutably grew in number and importance to them. Only one had left the family to find a different lifestyle.

Subsequent to receiving a Master's degree in college, RaNae's daughter was given employment in Missouri. It was her greatest joy to be given the opportunity to work in the agribusiness industry of Shelby County and live in a rural area. It wasn't long before she also made arrangements to move her two horses to settle into their new home. The horses, named Smoky and Beef, made their new residential move in an appropriate style. Four adults and a dog were in the entourage as two vehicles left Mississippi. One

21

vehicle was towing the horse trailer. They drove from Mississippi across a corner section of Tennessee into Missouri. It wasn't intended to be a race, so after a number of pauses en route for breaks and to check the animals' feed and water, all was well when they arrived about 11 hours later.

Being the resourceful and efficient person she is, RaNae could not allow the opportunity to pass without also adding some genealogy research on that trip. That expensive hobby was being pursued aggressively since her husband walked away. The day following the drive with Smoky and Beef, RaNae and her parents left the animals content in their corral and were off on the road again. That time they went south to the state capital, Jefferson City. Their search in the genealogical archives was made a pleasure as they found a little more information on one Clay Smith who seems to have been born about 1853 in Missouri. That dear man was found in the U.S. census of 1880, living in Kansas with two children and his wife, Elizabeth Black Smith. He was found to be an elusive farmer who didn't publish where he'd been, and he didn't leave forwarding addresses either. The information search on Granddad Clay was broken off for the day, and the researchers voiced their appreciation to the courteous state employees and left the city. They began the long drive back north to Shelbina to spend a second night with her daughter and the horses. The return drive's only interruption was a gasoline stop and a sandwich pause.

Plans were made to do some additional checking in St. Joseph, Missouri, on the following day. That next day, another long drive was made in a downpour in their search for Clay Smith. They parked the car at the Northwest Missouri Genealogical Society on Felix Street just after the noon hour and scurried inside out of the rain. RaNae paid the enrollment fee for membership and set about working with the books, charts, and lists. There were many records on births, marriages, divorces, deaths, cemeteries, U.S.

censuses, and more. One census record listed Clay Smith's father as being born in Pennsylvania and noted that his children were daughters aged three and five. The two days work did not yield much information for the elusive Clay Smith, and a third night was spent with RaNae's daughter after the drive back to Shelbina.

Slightly disappointed in their findings on the Clay Smith search, RaNae left the parents at the farm the next day as she accompanied her daughter to her work place. There, on a computer, she tirelessly searched for Illinois burial plots, cemeteries, and graveyard records, especially in Scott County, Illinois. She had bits of information about the parentage of her maternal grandfather who grew up as a foster child, never knowing his biological parents. Other relatives left some names and dates that established solid records of his family, but he never knew them nor had a childhood memory of his own parents. Without being adopted, he always kept his name.

With computer information, RaNae jubilantly returned to the farm near Shelbina for the fourth night's rest. She then convinced her parents that nothing should deter them in going to Winchester, Illinois, the next day. She had left off the paternal side of her family search only to look eastward across the state to Illinois for a country grave plot that reportedly had about 15 graves. It was only known on record as the Ellis family burial plot. It was said to be on a farmer's land four miles east of town.

On the fifth day after leaving Mississippi to move horses and dream of genealogical troves, RaNae and her parents left Shelbina again. They drove east on Missouri Route No. 36, crossing the Mississippi River into Illinois, where the highway became Interstate No. 72. That calendar date reminded her veteran dad that it was D-Day in Europe, 58 years later. Their target was the city of Winchester on an older Route No. 106. Locally, the folks called it the "hard top." The town's sign says, "Welcome to Historic Winchester."

Entering the town from one direction, the population is noted to be 1,700. From the other direction, the sign proclaims a population of 1,800, but those folks were found to be the friendliest folks imaginable.

Ready for a noon meal, RaNae and her parents were directed to the only family-style restaurant out on the "hard top." It was called Buck & Jo's Too, and they ate in the relaxed atmosphere at tables. A question was posed to the waitress about a certain farm out east of town. That was when she pointed to a table across the room where some senior gentlemen chatted together and drank coffee. "One of them can tell you," she said. RaNae took the answer as valid and introduced herself to the men, stating her mission. They answered her—talking two at a time—wanting to be helpful. In a brief moment, one said, "Go on and eat your meal. When you're through, I'll guide you out there." Excitedly, the amateur genealogists didn't tarry in finishing their meal.

In his pickup, the local resident named Wisdom led the way, taking the newcomers directly to a Mr. Rex Worrell's farm and introducing them to him and his wife, Marian. It was later in the afternoon that Mrs. Worrell told RaNae's mother that they had made their day. No kinder people were ever found than that congenial senior couple of Scott County, Illinois.

After stating their mission in small bits of information with few details, the newcomers listened to Mr. Worrell as he talked and pointed to a tiny wooded lot about 300 yards across a soybean field. The plot could have been about 30 by 40 yards, not exactly square. Mr. Worrell noted that it had been years since anyone had given the plot any attention. It was terribly overgrown with anything that would take root, even to big trees. That fact was obvious as the newcomers looked on from the short distance across the field.

With their car parked in the shade of Mr. Worrell's yard, the two women anxiously walked ahead while RaNae's father fingered with a camera and fell behind. Only pictures could properly record the existence of the family plot. It was so dense with growth that the ancient fence around the grave plot could be touched by the time one was close enough to see it. The cameraman had no kinship to those buried there, except by marriage. Catching up with the two women, he walked cautiously, knowing that snakes have no conscience or have any obligation to warn before they strike.

When the fence was found, he began to walk it, hoping to find a gate or place where he could climb over. RaNae nearly shouted as she gazed over the fence at one point through the brush to spy a stone marker with the name James M. Ellis, born Aug. 11, 1819. The man that discovered King Tut's tomb in Egypt wasn't any more thrilled than those two descendants of that man named Ellis. He was born when the U.S.A. was a fledging nation of only 35 years old. RaNae had found the grave of her great-great grandfather, preceding her in birth by five generations or nearly 140 years.

Her father found a place to cross the fence and began to break down and push aside enough tree limbs and brush to help her mother over the fence. He took her hand to assist her and then RaNae in crossing over the fence into the small cemetery. Once inside, the mother found a large stick to use as a club to help her through the brush.

On the inside, with the big club in hand, the mother rushed around like a child from stone to stone, calling out names and dates. RaNae and her father became busy digging out half-buried stones and placing them to be pictured, having to clean most in order to read the inscription. Some were so damaged with age and fractured by falling trees and/or other stones that every word was not legible. RaNae's father used up the film in one camera and began to use an auxiliary camera he had brought.

While he and RaNae worked as rapidly as possible, the mother was clubbing her way excitedly from grave to grave, each time announcing her newest find. A couple of times, the father paused long enough to chide with the mother for talking too loudly and going so fast that they could not keep pace with her. It isn't known if Mr. Worrell heard excited voices and came across the bean field to check, but for whatever reason, he was soon talking across the fence to whoever would answer him.

It was some time later when the three tired, dirty, and sweaty graveyard sleuths returned to their vehicle. They crossed the bean field to the country home where Mr. and Mrs. Worrell then awaited. Water was freely given to wash faces and hands, and the two women also removed shoes and washed their feet. It was then that Mrs. Worrell suggested that they could bathe in the house if they wished. Mr. Worrell went into the house and returned with photocopies of an abstract to the property deed to demonstrate when the property was first acquired from the U.S. Government. The year was 1800, and the purchaser named Lusby was an earlier kinsman to the Ellis family.

Three exuberant grave plot detectives left the Ellis burial place and the hospitality of the senior couple, as afternoon shadows grew longer. They drove back to town for another short delay at Buck and Jo's Too. They then drove off westward to retrace their route to Shelbina for a fifth night's lodging.

RaNae's maternal grandfather, William Walter Ellis, had never seen or known the location of any of what they had discovered that day. He lived to be nearly four-score years old. After starting in infancy as a foster child living in another family's home with their children, it would be folly to think that his many years didn't afford him lots of loneliness as he wondered who he was. In his experiences in life, he never became a son to any or a brother to none.

A forlorn lifetime of wonderment and unanswered questions afforded him no reprieve. His final escape came in a tiny bedroom of a nursing home in Arkansas where, in the end, his wife of 60 years visited him daily. News of his death distressed one of his daughters who wept 3,000 miles away on another continent. That daughter was the one that carried the big stick to beat away the brush from his grandfather's gravestone on D-Day, 58 years later.

RaNae's loneliness had taken a recess for a day. She had worked hard to rein in her family a little closer than before; therefore, she felt some achievement.

~~~~~~~~~~~~~~~~~~~~~~~~~~~~~~~~~~~~~

Lasting Name, Jimmy Woods

Written October 10, 1989

There was a time when railroad men with little seniority and growing families found themselves often visiting their favorite pawnshop. For some, it was every month; sometimes it was even more often. The visit invariably was to get a few dollars loaned on a watch or other personal item of value or a return to redeem it. There were two brothers, who were railroaders, who found themselves in their favorite pawnshop on a stormy night. This time they had come to buy an inexpensive used item—barber clippers.

The brothers reasoned together that they could be saving money to help their troubled economies by cutting each other's hair. They only needed the barber tools, so there in the pawnshop, they looked for a bargain. With a heavy rain falling on the outside and not too anxious to be getting wet, one of the two decided to make a phone call. Conveniently, there was a pay phone in the corner of the room, and the two huddled in the corner while one made his call.

The place was empty with little prospect for customers on such a bad night, but suddenly the door was pushed open. In marched a man, dripping wet. He probably had some cash earlier in the evening but had spent it with a drinking buddy. No doubt he had been a customer in the shop before, or at least he felt comfortable enough in his surroundings. The shotgun that he carried wasn't concealed; neither did he seem particularly threatening with it. However, it didn't escape the eyes of the two brothers in the corner, nor can they ever forget the audible sound that soon accompanied the visible.

Boldly the man with the shotgun marched up to the old-fashioned bank teller-style window. In a crisp voice of action he announced, "This is a holdup." The silence that fell became paralyzing fear. All was mute, and it dominated the shop. The huddled brothers in the corner feared that they were first witnesses and would become victims of something of which they didn't want any part.

The man with the gun either had second thoughts or a warped sense of humor. No one but he himself will ever know why, but suddenly he half dropped the gun on the small ledge of the bank teller window. "How much will you give me on my shotgun?" he asked. That dear relative of Gideon, the man in the Bible, came alive. In place of a shotgun scare, he came apart with a greater barrage of physical gestures and verbal expletives than anyone would have dreamed possible.

The brothers in the corner saw in that display of Jewish temper an avenue of escape. The brief action they witnessed didn't leave them with any curiosity or desire to keep hanging around. They made a fast departure out into the rain from the pawnshop.

As they hastily escaped, the brothers took something and left something. What they left was the bargain-priced barber tools, which they purchased later. What they took with them was the name of the would-be holdup man. He was contrite before his denouncer and begging. The brothers making the exit heard, "Awh, you know me, Mr. Cavenhaugh, I'm Jimmy Woods."

At the time of this writing, that stormy night scene is nearly 40 years in history, yet the vision of the shotgun and the memory of Jimmy Woods are very real.

~~~~~~~~~~~~~~~~~~~~~~~~~~~~~~~~~~~~~

Vondas A. Smith

Frozen In the Night

Written September 23, 1989

Prologue: Even if every family were to have in it a man or boy named John, there is one John that shall never be duplicated. This John was born early in the year of the great stock market crash—1929. He never joked about his memory, and for a fact, he had a good one. There was one time, though, that he over-extended himself. He began to chide with an older brother about how that brother could not remember when Herbert Hoover was President. President Hoover lost his second bid for office in 1932, about the time that John's parents were still rejoicing that he was out of diapers. In spite of it all, John still insisted that he remembered Mr. Hoover as President.

John was alive with ideas but none seemed to embrace a desire for education. After a struggle with a grade or two, he took a temporary leave from his school studies. He had a great love for God and his family, respect for the older generation, and an ability to wisely use his earnings. In these respects, one could write volumes about "good ole John."

No one ever boasted that John was a bold and fearless one. As a newlywed during the early 1950s, John parked his car one night in front of the Ferguson's Meat Company and entered to check on his brother's late working hours. Others waited in his car out front, including his wife and their mother. His brother's job title could aptly be called "bone and gut cleanup man." He was the last to leave the slaughterhouse, and since it was Saturday night, no one would be back until Monday morning to open up the business.

The older brother was hurriedly working, making numerous trips from the cutting floor to the large cooler room to store meat away, when John entered to visit. The large storage area had two entrances and was well lighted inside. It maintained a low temperature but was not freezing. Above each door was a small adjustable ventilator, but it was too small for a man to pass through.

Being too busy to stop to chat, the two walked together and talked about a probable hour to finish the work. They entered the cooler room with arms loaded with meat. That door had to remain open while being inside for there was no latch handle to operate the lock from within. However, John didn't know that, and he pulled the door shut. The click of the door startled John's brother who quickly turned to ask, "You didn't close the door, did you?" John's casual response was in the affirmative.

It wasn't immediately a big deal to John but the older brother was thoroughly stunned. He knew fully well that they were incarcerated. An idle minute passed without questions and answers while they looked intermittently at each other and then at the door. The temperature wasn't comfortable, and there was no place to sit or lie down. There wasn't anything to do but wait.

Reluctantly, they began to do just that in their awkward boldness. Snooping around in their newly acquired quarters, one clicked the light switch off and on. They began to eat wieners, count the hams, and then try the doors again. Not many minutes passed before a ton of despair moved in, and the whole load fell upon John. In response to his questions, he was told again that they could not rescue themselves, but rather someone else had to open the door from the outside.

John began to get noisy, and he wasn't connecting his thoughts and his expressions well. His brother had to get some diversionary action going because John was a man, and when he came apart, he was all over the place. The older brother embraced an idea that proved to be futile in helping them out of their winter-like quarters, but any suggestion readily had John's cooperation. They began to pull strips of wood from packing crates and use the rusty wire to fasten them into a pole. While standing on wooden boxes with handkerchiefs tied to the end of the flimsily fabricated pole, they thrust it through the ventilator above the door. This was done hoping to attract the attention of someone who wasn't there.

After fully a half hour, with hard-core fear and becoming colder all the while, John began to react with signs of hysteria. He had begun a replay of his reaction to exhaustion in the middle of the community center swimming pool back when he was about seven years old. In the cooler, he needed a rescuer again, and he began to call for one with all the fervor that he employed back then. At age seven he was straightway looking into the face of death by drowning. Now in his situation he could not visualize anything short of death for both of them as they waited out the weekend in the cooler room of a slaughterhouse. The older brother was playing it cool with his displayed emotions while the refrigerated temperature was also getting closer to his bones. By this time, he also was anxious for John's liberating angel.

The meat company still carried the name of the founder, but the widow had married again. The second husband was one that thoroughly enjoyed living. He drove a convertible automobile and extraordinarily enjoyed late-hour activities. There were times, and weekends occasionally made up some of those, that he needed to stay beyond Mrs. Ferguson's corrective reach. If the hour were late enough, sometimes he would go to his office at the meat company to sleep off some of his inebriation. It isn't known if Ross were divinely inspired or devilishly motivated, but on that Saturday night Mrs.

Ferguson's second husband found himself needing to become a recluse for a few hours. He sought the sanctuary of his office for some private time in search of an alibi and some strong coffee.

There was a crescendo of a distraught voice erupting from the locked-in quarters of the cooler room as Ross unlocked and entered the building. No one shall ever know the emotional feeling that seized his drunken mind by walking into a place occupied by an irrational human. Dead animals don't voice such a babble of incoherence. Without doubt, John was expressing some of Jonah's emotions when that prophet of God found himself in the fish's belly. Of course, the newly arrived went straight for the meat cooler room and snatched open the door. All bedlam ceased at once when John's angel appeared. With a voice laden with high decibel points, John erupted with, "Ross, am I glad to see you!"

No one would ever say that angels would become drunk, but to John, there is one drunk that became an angel on a hot July night while envisioning himself facing death in the cooler room of a meat packing house.

~~~~~~~~~~~~~~~~~~~~~~~~~~~~~~~~~~~~~

Vondas A. Smith

Wedding Tribute, First Daughter

Written February 25, 1972

On an evening 259 months ago, my wife, being large with her first child, announced joyfully and fearfully that her first pains in childbirth had arrived. On the following day, there was given to us the most precious gift that had ever been our joy to hold—our new baby. She was the first of five children, and the first grandchild to my dear parents. Tiny, beautiful, and abounding with health was this, God's gift.

Our joys multiplied by the days—there was the baby shower—and a few days later, on the Lord's Day at the morning worship hour, her mother and I stood meditatingly and prayerfully as we publicly presented her unto God. It was a ceremony, yes, but much more than words and signs. Her first pastor, Rev. T. Richard Reed, prayed earnestly the dedicatory prayer asking God's blessings spiritually, physically, and materially to be upon her in life.

There was the first tooth, her first words, and the first steps in walking that added to the blessings of parenthood. One bright morning, we assisted her in making the plunge into the great world of the unknown as she was introduced to her first grade teacher. She got her introduction into a school classroom's strange environment.

In infancy, before her knowledge of anything or anyone, her first music was heard in a worship sanctuary where she was involuntarily carried. Her first public presentation was in the congregation of the faithful. The first oratory to her hearing was the preaching of God's word from the sacred desk. Though involuntarily, as the beginning must be, she began her own personal dedication with a repented heart early in girlhood. Her baptismal burial in the name of Jesus was administered joyfully by these, my hands. Her Christian testimony recounts her personal experience of receiving the baptism of the Holy Ghost, evidenced by speaking in other tongues as the Spirit gave utterance.

Graduating from high school, then beginning work in public employment thrust her into a new roll of life with liberties and added privileges, yet she continued to be a faithful daughter, a Sunday school teacher, a member of the church orchestra, and of the family singing trio.

There were music lessons, recitals, church youth camps, and occasional family moves to a new address. This brought new schools and new friendships. All of this added both delight and difficulties through the years of Vonda's girlhood. There were highlights of summer vacations that brought joys, mutually enjoyed by Vonda and her sisters, brother, and we, the parents.

Almost 18 months ago, as plans had been made for Vonda's greater Christian education, she arrived on the campus of the Texas Bible College in Houston. Among the acquaintances that were soon made was one Howard Smith, with whom she now stands. That friendship grew, while at first they called one another cousin, since they have the same last name. With the passing of time, they began to find that they had more in common than the family name. The friendship matured, giving place to more intimate and sacred emotions. Recognizing their mutual love hence brought expressed desire, by each of them, to become united in marriage. This has afforded her mother, sisters, brother, and I the mutual joy and honor both to witness and participate in this most sacred rite tonight.

To have the honor to co-officiate with a fellow minister, Rev. H. V. Hodge, has added to my appreciation of this sacred hour.

To the bridegroom: You may step nearer to join the bride, and we shall continue with the marital ceremony.

Vondas A. Smith

Wedding Tribute, Second Daughter

Written June 1, 1973

The events leading to tonight had their beginning two decades and five months ago. It seemed so untimely—a cold December night, the demanding holiday season, and even the doctor was not in town. This second daughter, born on that night to her mother and I, had her happy introduction in a small hospital in a modest city not many miles from here. She was welcomed into our home by her proud and admiring 28-month-old sister. There were four of us then to grow together and share both the pleasant and difficult experiences of life.

Almost as quickly as her arrival, she had her introduction to the church's nursery department. There was the presentation in church and dedication to the Lord, asking for His blessing until she became of age to make her own consecration. The baby grew and matured too quickly. She was quiet, strong, peace loving, very pretty, and had an unusual love for dolls and pets. There was an inseparable bond between the new baby, Debbie, and her paternal grandmother. The grandmother sewed homemade dresses, gave private car rides, chewing gum, and her strong hand of affection and discipline made her a big girl before her years. It is as if she always walked and talked, almost without having to learn how. In her was a self-assurance and confidence that displayed itself with an almost reckless courage. This was seen on Christmas morning once at the age of seven when she announced her intentions to go skating on her new skates. The repeated falls were frustrating for she knew how to skate for sure, but the skates were out of order. She soon mastered the art of skating in spite of those bad skates.

During the next summer, Debbie wanted to display her swimming talent and jumped into the current of White River to prove it. She welcomed daddy's hand, though, as she was dragged from the river.

School was a dreaded chore for Debbie for there were more interesting things to do. Once as she enjoyed a good climb, she toppled from a wall and spent the following weeks recovering from a fracture. Real suffering came not until about four years ago when an overturned taxi left her with a painful back injury that brought many months of suffering.

There were some moves for her and the family bringing new schools and new friends to meet. Adjustments were easy enough but not always enjoyed. Music lessons brought her the position of church pianist in her father's pastorate of a new mission church at the age of 11. Music recitals, Vacation Bible Schools, and church youth camps enriched Debbie with excitement and experiences. Family vacations, church rallies, conventions, and General Conferences found Debbie a ready participant. Her Christian experience came early in life with repentance and baptism in the name of Jesus. When she received the Holy Ghost at the Tennessee youth camp, those Christian activities were endeared to our entire family. Later, a semester at the Gateway Bible College in St. Louis brought her many new friends and a greater appreciation of God's word.

A little more than a year ago, to us the parents, a holy unrest seized upon our hearts. Vonda Ruth had married, and when we should have become comfortable after the excitement, a door opened that led us into the sub-tropics of southwest Mexico. My unrest intensified, and it was shared by most of the family. We returned to Mexico some weeks later and met a near tragedy. I returned for a third trip, and almost as quickly as I arrived home, I gathered the family and visited the Foreign Missions Department of the United Pentecostal Church headquarters in St. Louis, Missouri. My resignation after 9 ½ years as founding pastor of our church found us soon to be centering our church worship activities here at the First U.P.C. The Christian fellowship was much needed and welcomed by my family and I. It was as if God had directed each step.

To most of our family, the foreign mission field seemed to loom near and real, and unanswered questions began to come uninvited. The "what about Debbie" began to be a matter of prayer and in His own time and place the Lord brought together the glance of two pair of youthful eyes. There was their meeting in a casual mood, and then a seeming mutual interest. A date brought subsequent dates, and infatuation grew to a genuine fondness. Who can tell at what time and place that the tender emotions of love were realized and expressed? Both you and I that are family and friends do not dare to tamper with those hearts that lock these secrets. Eternity will reveal all things, but enough is evident to unquestionably convince us that this young woman and this young man are truly in love.

For a second time in our life, my wife and I have been asked to relinquish our claim to a most precious trust. In regard to our daughters and son that God has given us, we do not expect that it shall ever be a painless occasion. So tonight, there stands in your presence this young woman, Debbie Smith, and this young man, Ricky McCarver, who plead the blessings of God and your favor upon their union as husband and wife. In behalf of her mother, her sisters, her brother, and I, we make this plea and enjoin you in prayer to this end.

Wedding Tribute, Third Daughter

Written August 1974

The sun was up on that March morning in 1955. I had finished my work shift on a cool night in the railroad yard, walked a few hundred yards, and boarded a slow-moving freight train leaving town north bound. Engineer C. W. Bowers was at the throttle of north bound train No. 134 as I mounted the lead unit of the engine. We were approaching the Mississippi River Bridge leaving Memphis, and I felt that I had to be on that train. Mr. Bowers ordered me off, and I obeyed, only to let a dozen freight cars pass me by before mounting a tank car for a 90-minute ride that took over two hours. The freight took a siding to meet a passenger train at Sedswick, and I left it to take to the highway. A farm tractor was going my way, so the young operator paused to let me on in a standing position on the back. As it began to rain, I felt tiredness sweep over me and thought about how things were not working out well in my favor. These 15 miles were backtracking for me because Engineer Bowers did not observe the street crossing laws of 15 mph as he went through the town of Jonesboro where I wanted to disembark. The engineer saw me when I jumped on the tank car, he knew where I was headed, and he deliberately went through town so fast that I couldn't jump off the railroad car. These were some of the things I thought, but one thing that I knew was that he was plain ornery.

I was so exhausted when I got to Mom's house that I stretched out on the couch in the living room and went to sleep. Noon was soon to come, but fatigue outweighed my hunger, so rest came first. My wife had been with Mom and Dad for some days, and birth was close for what I hoped would be our first son. The first pains were happy signs for us both, but untimely ones for the way I felt physically. It must have been early afternoon when Mom took Leah to the hospital. Shortly after, she returned the short distance to scold me for not rushing to be at the hospital to welcome our third little one.

I did get off to the hospital and found Leah in the labor room. There I started to do what I had done twice before. I prayed for a soon delivery, wished I could bear some of her pain, said all the sweet things that I'd said for nearly seven years of marriage, held her hand tight and waited, hopefully, fearfully, and tearfully. After some time, I was asked to make my way to another one of the hospital rooms, and the doctor was called. It was about 5 p.m.

Later, the smile of the doctor told me all that I wanted to know. All is over, and all is well. After the hours, even though they were not a great many, that message was really what I had prayed for and hoped for. When he said, "you have a girl," I almost forgot that I wanted a boy, and when I saw her pretty little self, I felt a need to apologize. My mother gave dad three boys and my wife gave me three girls. What a reversal! "Who cares," I thought, "that is if we can find a name?" My wife finally accepted the name of Llalanda after my two prior unsuccessful attempts with the other two daughters. RaNae was her additional name, and my father gave her the last name of Smith.

The third day was time to take her and her mother home. In the car, I had baby clothes that were new and used, pink and blue, given and purchased. A bassinet occupied the back seat as I drove toward the hospital that was yet 35 miles distant. It was checkout time, and I was late, but little did any of us know that I would never get there. Instead, those baby things were strewn in a collision. Over four months of my recovery gave the baby and I plenty of time together, and we really got acquainted. There was lots of time spent in the homes of family on both sides of her kinship. Nae and I started the same kind of acrobatics that was commonly done with the other sisters and I. We often walked to the store with her in arms and her sisters hanging on my pockets on either side. Her baldheadedness suggested to everyone for months that she might be our first son. She was our source of joy and consolation during one of the most difficult years of our lives. Attorneys, charges, courts, mortgage payments, and unemployment checks were unpleasantly with us, but we had a new baby. She didn't walk as soon as some, but neither did she get the chance. We all knew that babies don't walk. As she grew, many of her new dresses were those that her sisters didn't quite wear out.

No one shamed her about wet bed sheets in the morning because she decided on her own that there must be a better way. To her, it was to slide off the bed until her dangling legs found the floor. In this accommodating position, it was convenient and comfortable, and saved getting the bed wet.

The same preacher's hands that baptized her mother and I, performed our wedding ceremony, and held her sisters in dedication prayer, also offered Llalanda RaNae Smith to the Lord in dedication prayer. Llalanda was too hard to say for her sisters so they simply said Nae Nae. I added a loving bit and called her Nae Bob. A few teeth later, after lots of crawling, and a head of blond curly hair still short enough to be thought to be a boy, she set out into the big world of her front porch walking alone at age one. She soon learned more than many folks are able to learn in a lifetime. Worms, frogs, and all but a few bugs don't bite. Frogs are more fun by the dozen, especially if they're hidden in a pocket of the car. If those little hands that put them there were to forget them, Dad finds them later, too late for their survival. A mouse was most interesting to her at five, when she once showed her mother her prize catch.

On the day of her fifth birthday, she arose with the mumps. The Lord blessed the day with a five-inch snow, and I made her a snowman to view

41

from her window. After recovery, she began again to beat a path in the spring grass going across a back lot to the store nearby for popcicles. These she always shared with her baby sister who sat in the back door in her high chair to await her return with popsicles.

In her long dress (a favorite style) and high-heeled shoes, she was always the teacher while playing school. Her baby sister was now talking, saying more intelligible things than "iggie-biggie-boogie-bigga-pigga-baya." Her mother broke a secret to her one day that she was going to have a little brother or sister, and what could have made Nae Bob happier? The prospect of having another one to join her play school was promising to her career. In her sixth year, a move to Memphis from Newport, Arkansas, brought new neighbors, new friends, a new church, and her first real school.

As we sat at breakfast one morning after moving to Memphis, I talked to the older sisters about marrying a Christian for a husband. I assured them that I'd help them find a good husband, and Nae Bob broke in to say, "Daddy, find me a husband, too."

Too soon for her mother and me, we began to see her toys abandoned. The dolls lay in the closets more and more as the wheels of skates and bicycles began to appeal to her. During childhood, as some reckon the years, she made her repentance of sin to follow the Lord Jesus, was baptized in His name, and received the Holy Ghost in December before she was 10 years old. Her play church was recognized by our God and made to become her real experience of life. The plain dress gave way to prettier styles, there were new tastes in shoes, and then the nylons all spoke of young lady hood. Books became more fascinating, and school was serious business. The honor roll was meant to be commonplace. A musical instrument was chosen to play in the church band. Youth camps and family vacations occupied the summers. She took on a new roll of leadership to become counselor of girls during the Junior Youth Camps in Tennessee. Nae reached the roll of Who's Who of American High School graduates in the year of her graduation. She declined to accept available scholarships with an eye that looked toward Latin America. In the mean time, she became a clerk in the store where her mother worked and didn't cease to astound the other employees by being able to be a buddy with her own mother. Though strange in the family style of today, she was a loving daughter and sister, thus winning affection to her. Her unassuming and unselfish desires were portrayed in a letter to Santa in which she once wrote, *"Dear Santa, to buy all I want for Christmas, it will cost $13. 21—but you don't have to get me anything. By, RaNae. P.S. I am sorry if you are ill and cannot come."*

The saddest experience in the beginning of her memories was the burial of her paternal grandmother when Nae was nearly 3 ½ years old. Arriving two months later, the little brother that she might have wanted, became her third sister. She joined all the others of the family to give the baby enough room in our growing family and more than enough attention. She was forbidden to date until age 16, for it is a family tradition. Friends were plentiful, letter writing was to her a pleasure, and her mail came frequently.

I will forever feel that the sincere persuasion of her presence, even to include tears, were known and seen of God who moved the hearts of those men on the Foreign Mission Board last October in Salt Lake City. The decision of the church board seemed to affect the future of RaNae as a member of the missionary family. Very soon, unaware to any of us, the will of God in His great wisdom was going to change unexpectedly the future for all of us. For some weeks, over 5,000 miles and in many churches, she and I traveled together close enough to hold hands, but I was becoming increasingly aware that at times she was far away. She was kind, hard working, and praying with me for the promotion of Bolivian evangelism. An occasional phone call home, many letters, and tears told only part of the complete story. The secrets of the heart seek to be revealed, and though had I been told plainly that she was in love, I perhaps was too busy to have understood, had I even listened. After her travel role was replaced to become more of a keeper at home, her mother and I began traveling together. The holidays of Valentine's Day, Easter, Mother's Day, Father's Day, and a few birthdays, quickly brought the charming month of June.

It was early in June, while we were in northern Maine, when a letter was handed to me. This letter, from the bridegroom standing with us tonight, brought a mixture of anger, disappointment, and sorrow. In my frustration over that appealing letter, I purposely waited until I was able to think more rationally before attempting to answer. I wrote a letter in a reply that I never signed nor was it mailed. I prayed for wisdom, sought patience, and hoped for the will of God. I may never know how happy I am for keeping my first emotions at least to the point to where it cannot be damaging to the union of these that are so in love. Little did I know when writing this letter that I would mention parts of it publicly in a kind of confession of an error that I almost made. I read from the letter:

"I received your letter only yesterday that dealt quite honestly concerning your proposal to RaNae and seeking the consent of her mother and me. I should have gotten it Sunday afternoon, but my wife thought she was doing me service to keep it from me until after the weekend. I do appreciate your honest approach and sincerity and feel that you've showed some due respect, but it is ironic that this came at a time when we were the farthest from home. I am not saying, though, that distance has been the one situation causing me to feel as I do. In the event that I were able to

44

determine that Nae is putting you under a feeling of urgency in the marriage, then I owe you the respect of a friend, and her the wisdom of a father in voicing disapproval. If the reverse is true, then I can only plead with you on the basis of reasoning. The relationship between you two was friendship when I was last with RaNae, and she has mentioned, upon questioning, that her plans were to go to Bolivia and attend college. This is a rare opportunity that I'm sure you would appreciate and would want Nae to have. This sudden thought of marriage seems to be an abandonment of plans that were once carefully thought out and dear to her. You will be faced with the reality that she would be paying a tremendously big price, which may put you in a position of disadvantage at some time in your marriage. It is not possible for me to object to a marriage because of you as a person, for we both know well that we are not truly acquainted with one another, nor have I met any of your family. To object to you would be an unfair judgment, but to object to a marriage at this time on the basis of what I know, seems the only course that I can conscientiously take."

I never signed this letter, nor did I or could I mail it. Happily, I kept it to myself until this very hour. How could I know at what time and place that the exchange of a glance gave birth to an infatuation and this spawned the first emotions of an endeared relationship? Known only to our God is the point in this relationship that love was first realized. As you stand together here tonight, it may seem more probable that you have been forever in love.

Both you and I that are family and friends do not dare to tamper with those hearts that lock love's secrets. Eternity will reveal all things, but enough is evident to unquestionably convince us that this young woman and this young man are truly in love. For a third time in our life, my wife and I have been asked to relinquish our claim to a most precious trust. In regard to our daughters and son that God has given, we do not expect that it shall ever be a painless occasion. So tonight there stands in your presence this young woman, Llalanda RaNae Smith, and this young man, Walter Glenn Vaughn, who plead the blessings of God and your favor upon their union as husband and wife. In behalf of her mother, her sisters, her brother, and I, we make this plea for your blessings and enjoin you to prayer to this end.

~~~~~~~~~~~~~~~~~~~~~~~~~~~~~~~~~~~~

Wedding Tribute, Fourth Daughter

Written April 7, 1982

Since she was born our fourth daughter, she came at a most appropriate time to brighten her new home. Less than two months before her birth, her paternal grandmother was buried. It had been more than 3 ½ years since the birth of her youngest sister. So with the other three children no longer babies, and coming to a family saddened by the first death in the immediate family, her arrival was received with great joy. Her name, Julia LeiRene, is a selection of names remembering her mother (Leah), grandmother (Irene), and great-grandmother (Julia).

She immediately had four mothers when you take into account that her three older sisters were in constant attendance to her every need. She smiled easily and won the hearts of all that knew her. She wasn't a baby very long, for no sooner had she begun to walk, she could be seen wearing a huge, over-sized dress belonging to her 8-year-old sister or even an old pair of her mother's shoes. In addition to her love for her big family and her many friends, she had a wholesome devotion for food. This kept her plump and healthy.

For almost the first 18 months of her life, she did not enjoy the luxury of having her family unit together. Her dad's pastoral duties and secular employment in a different city to maintain the growing family found them apart five days per week. Only on the weekends did they enjoy the pleasure of being together as a family.

The years passed too quickly. During that wonderful time of girlhood, many friends touched her life. There were pets and toys, there were vacations to enjoy, and there were pictures to record those fond memories. During those years of school, childhood playing, music study, and the many activities that are so pleasurable, she arrived one day to have to make a most serious decision. That simply was whether or not she would choose to become a follower of our Lord Jesus Christ or follow after the things of this world. She demonstrated superior intelligence when she kneeled in repentance before our Lord to confess her sins and her need for His divine guidance for the rest of her life. Having been baptized in His name, she then received the baptism of the Holy Ghost in a summer youth camp of the church.

After having become a young lady, she found herself swept away from her way of life. Some 7 ½ years ago, she was introduced to a new continent, a new culture, and a new language. She adapted well and has become content, so content that she has fallen in love with her new way of life. That love has now included a young man whom she wishes to share all the remaining experiences of her life, be they pleasurable or difficult. Mutually, the two have a most important experience in common; that is their faith in God and devotion to His service. Adding to this, their love for one another will enable them to surmount every obstacle that may threaten their unity in holy matrimony.

Her parents once saw her as a baby of 53 centimeters, weighing 3.95 kilos, but tonight they must accept the realities that confront them. She, LeiRene, is an adult, and has now found a love that is about to bind her life to that of her lifetime companion. Those parents, her mother Leah and I, have accompanied her for these first 23 years of her life, and we now find it to be both joyous and sad to have come to this final moment to give her in marriage.

These two, Jorge and LeiRene, know the seriousness of this occasion. They understand that Christian marriage is until death. On this occasion, the most solemn and important decision that two adults will ever be called upon to make together, they have come to make public that decision in your presence. They wanted the presence of their friends and brethren of the faith to witness this sacred occasion.

You that are present, will by your presence and attendance, make this hour a memorable one for this dear couple, the parents of the bride, and those family members of the groom. In behalf of the families of both bride and groom, let me say thank you for having come, and we welcome you sincerely.

~~~~~~~~~~~~~~~~~~~~~~~~~~~~~~

Vondas A. Smith

Weary Deputation

Written May 1988

<u>Prologue</u>: This and other writings were lost to the author when his word processor was taken from his burglarized home in Bolivia, South America, in November 1988. However, his granddaughter, Karisha Vaughn, returned this copy to him. It had been given to her during her vacation with her grandparents while they were traveling in California in July 1988.

Missionary preacher, Bible teacher, road away from home,
The day he's hired is the one he's fired and left so much alone.
Starts a new day with a pause to pray, asking for his bread,
And without a shame he ends the same, hoping for a bed.

Going by train, be it a plane or a van with its trailer,
Motor home buff, hiking it rough, or taking a boat like a sailor.
He continues to go, hoping to show, his burden for a people,
Trying to smile all the while, he's thinking of the needful.

Too proud to cry, too young to die, he hides some deep emotion,
Burdened in heart for a part of the world not knowing devotion.
There's just a part of all his heart he shares with his neighbor,
Who would never hear of his fear of age when he cannot labor.

Missionary preacher, Bible teacher, the road is his home,
If today he's hired he's also fired, so he lives by faith alone.
Tomorrow, a new day when again he'll pray, for a portion of bread,
And trust without shame he can end the same, by finding another bed.

~~~~~~~~~~~~~~~~~~~~~~~~~~~~~~~~~~~~

Fear of the Second Year

Written after a year of deputation in the U.S., 1988

Deputation, foreign nation, a little fuss and cry,
Desperation, with frustration, a year has now gone by.
I thought for fun, while on the run, to write some words of rhyme,
While looking ahead, without a dread, to make this church on time.

"Tell me, dear, where to from here," asks the she of he?
"Don't rightly know, let's crank and go, we're running behind you see.
Do your face, close up the case, don't leave the kids behind,
Let's rush, my dear, for I fear this place'll be hard to find.

My notes, my notes, well, bless my goat, where did I put the pad?
But goody for me, my memory will serve me better than bad.
Go a hundred north and forty south, a little east and west,
Just follow the sun with a run; let's leave nothing to guess.

I was told on the phone to really hold on, slow down in town,
At the light to hang a right, go up the hill and down.
Cross the bridge and top the ridge, look for a herd of swine,
You'll know of course, seeing the horse, you're near the county line.

Swerve with the curve, tee to the right, the railroad there you'll spot,
Go over the pass, if you need gas, there's the place to stop.
Be patient from here, 'cause you're near, it's tricky yet, you know,
Stay with the trail and don't fail, stay up with the traffic flow.

If you see a sign just keep in mind, follow this easy instruction,

Just look ahead to water's edge, that'll be your only obstruction.

Don't get lost at any cost, preacher don't fear, for you're nearer,

Quickly now, you'll start to smile, you need only to cross the river.

Deputation, foreign nation, a little fuss and cry,

Desperation, with frustration, a year has now gone by.

I thought for fun, while on the run, to write these words of rhyme,

While looking ahead without a dread, to make this church on time.

~~~~~~~~~~~~~~~~~~~~~~~~~~~~~~~~~~~~

Monkey Business

Written November 24, 1989

<u>Prologue</u>: Viewpoints and opinions are tenaciously held by some, however popular they may be. One of those strong opinionated conservatives had his wife and three little girls out shopping one afternoon. His railroad paycheck had just been cashed, and to them it was just like a holiday.

On the corner of Lamar and Airways in Memphis, Tennessee, was a large shopping center. It was relatively new, and one of the very fine businesses located in the shopping center was Katz Drug Store. There was a very fine pet department located in the basement of that drug store. The parents with the little girls were always compelled by the children to make a visit to see the pets. That afternoon they were again with the mice, birds, fish, puppies, and many others of the animal kingdom, even including monkeys.

The railroad man, employee of the Frisco Railroad, supplemented his income by driving new cars off the river transport barges brought down the Mississippi by tugboats and docked at the foot of Beale Street. That part-time work brought him into company of some younger men. It was first from those young drivers that he heard about a particular truck driver about town. He was a young fellow that had become the topic of conversation for so many local folks during that time. The talented youth with his guitar was packing out the nightclubs with his appearances and was doing so well that he didn't drive a delivery truck any more.

The new entertainer's name was beginning to show up in print. It was necessary only to mention his first name, Elvis, in order to get the attention of ready hearers. Those stories and little news bits, true or imaginable, were plentiful. Elvis was the admired, kind, benevolent victor in everything in which he was associated.

In the pet department of the Katz Drug Store that afternoon, the three small girls and their parents were admiring all the pet animals. Down the steps came unnoticed a young man flanked by another couple of able-bodied young men. The reason for three could be anyone's guess, but only one of them was meant to be the attraction. A description of his attire would defy almost anyone's effort. His shoes were of one color, his trousers were another, and the shirt was still another. He was plump but not fat, almost big enough to be threatening, if he were to become angry. He asked a clerk to show him a particular monkey from a cage. As quickly as he asked for the monkey and had it cradled in his arms, there was an elated shriek from a teenaged girl. Almost instantly, he was surrounded by other youth that included boys and girls. In little flirtatious touches to the girls on the head or shoulders, the spectacularly colorfully dressed youth, known to them as Elvis, did not ignore any of his admirers. That railroader, out with his family, didn't survey the newly arrived pet store gathering very long. To his wife he said, "Get the girls, and let's get out of here."

It has now been more than 3 ½ decades since that family walked out, leaving a group of admirers with their hero. That same strong opinionated daddy hasn't yet apologized for snatching his girls from possibly having the caressing hand of the King of Rock gently brush them on the head.

The tragic and ignominious passing of the King of Rock, with drugs flowing through his veins, is a sad commentary left to the memory of his millions of admirers. He earned millions and entertained millions and was colorful in song and movies. His benevolence and generosity was genuine and attested to. To that aging father of the little girls, who was zealous for their well being, a question comes to mind occasionally. "If lots of moms and dads had sheltered their children from the handsome youth in the center, would that young man have come to his demise quite so early in life?"

Not only did a pet store clerk put a monkey in Elvis' arms, millions of people put the showbiz monkey on his back.

~~~~~~~~~~~~~~~~~~~~~~~~~~~~~~~

Vondas A. Smith

Vernon, Flat Broke

Written November 30, 1989

Prologue: The Whitehaven area lay south of the city of Memphis, Tennessee, and extended down to the Mississippi state line when Sadnov bought his new, four-room house at 541 Sanford Road. The area enjoyed its own water district and Fire Department, and the Shelby County Police Department maintained law and order. Had the area been able to incorporate under state law as a city, it would have been the fifth largest city in Tennessee.

There were no mammoth shopping centers in Whitehaven in those earlier days of the 1950s. In some places, fields were still being cultivated. On U.S. Highway 51, leading south from Memphis, there was a big track of land owned by a doctor. He seemed to be a lover of horses for there were always some in the pasture.

Sadnov was a preacher that primarily supported his family by public employment. However, he would not let time escape without involving himself in his ministry. His church activities were kept within driving range of home and work, and some 10 years of ministerial experience were added to him during that time living in Whitehaven. In addition to a few positions of responsibility, he had also built a church in Arkansas.

During those years, modernization brought expressways, shopping centers, and lots of new housing developments into the country south of the city. A guitar-strumming entertainer out of Memphis bought the horse farm on Highway 51. Along with the community changes, Sadnov and his family were having some changes of their own.

It would seem that Sadnov's family was large enough with their four children, but the day came when there was an announcement of the fifth on the way. The family debt was becoming more difficult to maintain, the car was worn out, and now another baby was expected. Sadnov's problems weren't insignificant, so it necessitated a big step to meet the challenge.

He and his faithful wife began to draw in the reins. There was no alternative but to bring their activities closer to home. The little house was placed on the market and sold. Sadnov's cousin, wanting to move, gave over their bigger house for payment of closing costs and taking up mortgage notes.

There in the living room of the bigger house, Sadnov began anew in a mission church. The small beginning happily grew. After a time they moved into the Thomas B. Davis branch of the YMCA for weekend meetings. Property was then purchased on Raines Road not far from the old horse farm that had long since been named Graceland by the guitar entertainer, Elvis. By that time his humble origins were all but forgotten, and his wealth had moved up front.

The new church group at 929 East Raines Road found it necessary to construct a new church building and destroy the older building they had occupied for a time. Funds were scant, and loans were all but impossible to obtain. That was when Sadnov began to draw ideas out of experiences. Indeed, he once had a secondary involvement in the promotion and sale of church bonds, and this seemed to him the only route to pursue.

The legal work was drawn up, proper registration was made, bonds were printed, and everything was in perfect order to start selling the first mortgage bonds that earned six percent on the investment. Almost simultaneously, a contractor was chosen and work quickly began. The bonds were printed in denominations of $50 to $1,000, and that placed them in the buying range of almost everyone.

One day in the winter of 1969, a big payment was coming up for the contractor, and there was little money on hand. Sadnov had to move some bonds. It was a cold morning, and without announcing his plans or awaiting invitations, he took his briefcase and went out going straight to Graceland.

There was a winding driveway that led directly off the highway leading uphill to the house. The keeper at the gate was named Smith, and he had a small gatehouse to the right of the driveway. He came to the door, and Sadnov identified himself and stated his business. "You came at a bad time, sir," said Mr. Smith. "Mr. Elvis Presley has gone to Las Vegas, and I don't know when he'll be back," he added. "His father, Mr. Vernon Presley, is here. I just talked to him by phone a few minutes ago, and he is going out. He should be here in about five minutes. Wait, and you can talk to him," suggested Mr. Smith.

Sadnov, the bond seller, and Mr. Smith chatted the few minutes in the close-quarters of the warm gatehouse. The view from his vantage point showed that the chauffeur-driven Cadillac soon came slowly down the drive. Mr. Vernon Presley, sitting in the back, lowered the window enough to speak. He was immaculately dressed, spoke pleasantly, and was courteous enough to listen to Sadnov. His reply came as if it were already programmed. It was decisively spoken as he continued to be courteous and maintain his dignity.

"I'm terribly sorry, sir," said Mr. Presley. "I am unable to make any investment at this time. I've already invested what I have, and I'm broke," he continued. With that disclosure, he and his chauffeur moved out into the traffic on the highway.

A few blocks south in a shopping center, Sadnov's wife worked as a clerk in Fred's Dollar Store. She knew clerks in other stores in the vicinity, and it wasn't uncommon that the clerks exchanged stories about the wealthy neighbors that occupied the mansion called Graceland. One story came from a clerk at a Woolworth's Store and was told to Sadnov's wife.

The story was that Mr. Presley had bought a birdcage and taken it home. After a few days, he returned the cage and asked for his refund. On the refund slip was a blank to fill out the reason the customer wasn't fully satisfied with his purchase. "And why are you not happy with the purchase, sir?" asked the clerk. Mr. Presley replied, "My bird died."

The church bond salesman had felt a little badly for having been turned down by Mr. Presley, but what he learned later gave him reason to feel better about it. "He surely is a poor man," he mused. The salesman moved on and sold the bonds elsewhere and finished the church building at 929 East Raines Road.

~~~~~~~~~~~~~~~~~~~~~~~~~~~~~~~~~~~~~~

Vondas A. Smith

A German Who Wasn't a Nazi

Written October 10, 1989, La Paz, Bolivia

When Hitler was consolidating his power in Germany, Mr. Jensen was a young man. He was intelligent, ambitious, and loved the Boy Scouts and his work in that organization in his native country. However, the rising Nazi political dominion in Germany did not appeal to him. Then an opportunity opened up for him to go to Bolivia, South America, to work with his beloved Boy Scouts organization. It was there that he spent the rest of his life.

In 1985, after more than 50 years in Bolivia, Mr. Jensen sat behind his desk as one of the principal directors of a big company. Their business was paper products—school and office supplies. Although Mr. Jensen had long since left his Boy Scouts work, he maintained his Scouts' oath at heart.

During 1985, inflation in Bolivia, according to the *Wall Street Journal*, reached 45,000 percent for a time. On every prominent street corner in the capital city, people stood with pockets bulging with near worthless Bolivian paper money, wanting to buy U.S. dollars. With futile efforts, the police arrested those seeking dollars. Nevertheless, the dollar buyers multiplied, only hoping to rescue a little of their life savings. The government closed all the legal money exchange houses. However, the exchange houses only went under ground setting up business in alleyways or on upper floors of big buildings. Only regular customers who were scrutinized by a peephole in the door gained access for business.

An American woman named Ruth was living in Bolivia during those very troublesome times. It was a serious offense to be caught dealing with the street money exchangers, but her money only came through a checkbook account in the United States. Only the greenback currency of the U.S. was deemed of any value for street exchange.

It isn't really known how Ruth and Mr. Jensen came to know one another in those difficult days. For sure, it was the financial anarchy that ruled the streets that brought them together. He needed dollars for importation payments, and she needed the most in money exchange to cope with the daily morning and evening price increases.

The kind-hearted Mr. Jensen spoke several languages. He would engage his English when Ruth entered his office on the upper floor of his business building on Colón Street in downtown La Paz. She was one among numerous regular customers with her checkbook in dollars wanting to buy Bolivian pesos.

On one particular day, Mr. Jensen was reminiscing in casual chat with Ruth. Americans living abroad know other Americans in their vicinity, as do other nationalities know their own people living about them, too. Mr. Jensen knew all the prominent Germans and had interest in them and the culture they shared in common. There was one German man that had betrayed his real identity to Mr. Jensen, and he told the story.

Ruth heard from the old Scouts leader that a troubled friend entered his office once and wanted some advice. The frightened visitor to Mr. Jensen's office told his plight in a hushed, conversational voice. He ended his story by saying that he was a wanted man and had cause to fear that foreign agents knew his identity. "What would you suggest that I do?" questioned the old friend. The big benevolent German, Mr. Jensen, was legitimate all the way. He had nothing to fear. He had successfully escaped Nazi Germany, done well in business, and loved people. "Tell me, just who are you, if you are someone I don't know," asked Mr. Jensen. "I'm wanted in Israel, and in life I was the Nazi, Adolph Eichmann," was the reply. "Friend,

I suggest you leave Bolivia immediately," said Mr. Jensen. "This government administration will sell you in a minute," he added. The Nazi soon left for Argentina where agents of Israel later captured him. Subsequently, he was tried for crimes against humanity, convicted, and executed in Israel. His ashes were then spread over the Mediterranean.

Just as Ruth was about to leave Mr. Jensen's office, he asked a parting question that displayed a humanitarianism that isn't fitting to this generation. "Why do they keep hunting old Nazis like animals who now want nothing in the world but to finish living out their lives in peace?"

Epilogue: Mr. Jensen departed this life by natural causes in La Paz, Bolivia, about April 1989. There is little doubt that he knew others, less fortunate than himself, who followed him to Bolivia after becoming collaborators with Hitler in Nazi Germany. It isn't known if his question was ever answered to his satisfaction.

Men's Brown Shoes

Written September 25, 1989, La Paz, Bolivia

With her tiny Latin stature, ready smile, and a most pleasant personality, Maria was one young woman that could not easily be forgotten. Her English was good, even if it did come with an accent as big as an elephant. She had graduated in Houston as a foreign exchange student from Bolivia, South America, and then returned to her country. She was not a Catholic, but she was devout in her Christian faith. Once she spent three nights in jail after having been apprehended with some others while they were in a religious meeting. Their meeting was thought to have been a political rally by the powers that prevailed in her country during those times. It was at that time that her father, a dentist, informed her that her religion had gotten her into jail, and it could now get her out. She never grew bitter toward her dad for making that remark.

A little more than four years after completing high school, Maria was back in the United States, again in Houston. She was enrolled that time in a bible school. An opportunity presented itself for her to attend a church conference during her bible school days, and she conveniently found a family with whom she could ride. The distant drive to the conference took two days in addition to a night in a motel. During the day on the road, there were personal needs that called for stops. It was during one of these stops that Maria hurriedly found the rest room. Another of the family, the husband, was slower in walking to the restroom. He found the men's room and entered.

On the inside of the men's room there were individually partitioned stalls, and he occupied one of them. It would have been possible to look over the partition had one needed to, but that would have taken a little effort.

Anyway, who cares who is in the next stall? The effortless way to spy on the party next door was to look down at his shoes. He didn't even do that.

The husband to the family must have coughed, grunted, or sighed. At any rate, there was a sudden shuffling of feet in the stall next to him. That was when he spied the smallest pair of shoes imaginable for a man to be wearing. Those tiny shoes didn't tarry long and were gone almost as quickly as the cough.

Two or three minutes later the husband returned to the car to find Maria and his wife in a huddle. Their faces were long and displayed a certain degree of disbelief, almost fright, as each listened to the other's comments. As the husband was getting into the car his wife was heard to ask, "And what color were his shoes?" "They were big brown ones," said Maria. One dear wife looked at her husband's shoes and solved a mystery that calmed the fears of the little Latin girl who wore such tiny ones. No one knows who found the wrong door, but it began to seem that it was quite unimportant who occupied the stall next door.

Passing Washington Park

Written November 30, 1989

Prologue: Steve had lived in Venezuela for a number of years and spoke Spanish fluently. He had been an amateur boxer as a youth in the United States, and his more than six-foot frame was excellently proportioned. He was still under 40 years of age and good looking.

When Steve returned to the United States with his family, he took a ministerial position in New York City to work among the Latinos. He acquired a large theater building, which was no longer in business, and converted it into a church.

Marcus was an only son, 13 years old, and his parents were on their way to South America under appointment as missionaries. During a time of promotion, preparatory to leaving the United States, Marcus' parents visited Steve in the New York City theater church. The experience was enlightening and truly memorable. Steve and Marcus became immediate friends, and that friendship earned Marcus and his parents the favor of being special guests.

There were lots of interesting sights to see and places to go in the Big Apple. In the short time available during those two days of visit, Steve took Marcus and his parents to see some interesting places. One evening they decided to take an elevator tour of the Empire State Building. They ascended up 89 floors—as far as that elevator went—and from there they viewed other landmarks such as the World Trade Center and out over the harbor to the Statue of Liberty. The list of names and places grew long.

It isn't known if Washington Park was on the visiting agenda, or if it just became convenient to pass that way. Again it isn't known if the activities, occurring on that night in the park, were the nightly normal or perhaps a special occasion. Whichever it might have been—to prepare newcomers—it should forever be a prerequisite to forewarn the unsuspecting majority. That would be a necessity in order to take some of the edge off the tremendous shock.

Since the advent of AIDS back in 1981, there can be no doubt that some of what was viewed on that night has changed. What Marcus witnessed, under the lights and from the slowly moving car, could scarcely be recounted. Except to the minority of males who want to be something other than what God made them, the "goings on" that night could only be viewed as frightening.

All were what they were, but some appeared to be what they weren't. Those that appeared to be what they weren't surely had two wardrobes. One was for the he, and the other for the she, or be it that one was for the day and the other for the night. Life for them has to be an interesting one because they dedicate so much to it. Just imagine all the color blending of clothes, hair, face painting, and fingernails. They do superbly well with making the shoulders narrower at night and hips broader. Just think of those big aching feet in the night shoes with open toes and high heels.

There was no circus atmosphere, and no one was clowning around. It was serious business, and all were meticulously dedicated to whatever they proposed to be doing. All seemed to be adult enough to have had plenty of experience. They were divided into pairs sitting tightly embraced or laying on the ground. There were those with long hair, and those with it cut short. Some were kneeling facing each other with hand in hand and lips to lips. Less than half of them carried purses, but they were visibly present.

Whatever they talked about seemed to be in whispers, because silence prevailed. In the lifestyle of their choice, one would hope that their romancing and family planning never included children. It has never been known that a male has conceived.

One pass about the park in the automobile was sufficient. Steve with his family and Marcus with his folks had little or nothing to say. They certainly weren't taking the occasion to be making fun of what they beheld. For the most part, what they saw left them speechless or perhaps too breathless for speech. They drove away.

Silence prevailed in the car for a time, and it was Steve who finally spoke out to break the spell. He used his native tongue of English to speak to Marcus who knew nothing about Spanish. "Marcus," he said, "Whenever you start to carry a purse, you cease to be my friend." Marcus was irritated at the suggestion that he might ever want to do such a thing.

~~~~~~~~~~~~~~~~~~~~~~~~~~~~~~~

Vondas A. Smith

High-Flight Memories

Written December 12, 1998

Having taxied out on the runway of the La Paz International Airport on Bolivia's Altiplano, the big Boeing 757 lunged forward for departure. The runway was unbelievably long because of the distance needed to become airborne from the ground level of a 13,000-foot altitude. For the nine-hour flight to Miami, there was only one stop. This was in Santa Cruz at the modern Viru Viru Airport. A man and wife settled back for the daylong flight returning to the United States. Their first time to make such a flight between the United States and Bolivia had occurred over 24 years before. The Bolivian rain season was just beginning, and the approaching summer was less than two weeks away. The winter season was nearing in the U.S., and the couple was hoping that they were appropriately dressed for the seasonal change.

In a little less than an hour, the plane was on the ground again in Santa Cruz. Some passengers disembarked, and others embarked destined for Miami, the next stop. A big, strong-looking North American took the empty seat at the window in the row with the man and wife who boarded in La Paz. If a shave and haircut were needed to prepare a man for an international trip, that man left Bolivia unprepared. He called himself Pittman. Pittman was from Mississippi, and he was an oil field worker on assignment in Bolivia near the city of Villa Montes. He was almost too big for the space allotted the passengers in the economy section of the plane. The two men sat hours next to one another without knowing which language to use, if they had decided to talk.

The first man was an older retired gentleman who was returning from Bolivia with his wife after a 10-day visit to La Paz. He and his wife had been former Bolivian residents for nearly 23 years, and for more than 17 of those years, they had lived in the city of La Paz. Since the oil field employee was trying to be comfortable and get some rest, the older man regressed into thoughts and memories of many years ago when they first arrived in Bolivia without speaking the Spanish language.

His visit back to Bolivia was an experience in nostalgia. Some of the visions of yesteryears were pleasant, even very pleasant. All of it, however, was not that way. For years there had been a siege of government overthrows by military strongmen that brought army tanks, gunfire, and gas attacks into the streets. There were also many deaths. Blood stained the cobblestone streets too often to be forgettable. Dogs were used to restrain and control rioting university students and teachers. Tin miners seemed bigger and more ferocious in those days. He closed his eyes with a thought that was almost audible. "I've got to look to the lovelier days and the good memories in order to sense some peace here in this wind-tossing altitude of 35,000 feet."

He fought to forget the night he was helped from his overturned jeep and emerged out of the glass with a shoe in his hand to be carried off to the hospital for X-rays. He was alone that time. He was a passenger on a rain-slicked, muddy road in the jungles of Beni once when the vehicle, out of control, left the roadway for the jungle and suffered a shattered windshield and other damage. The millions of mosquitoes were too intimidating to make him want to leave the vehicle. "Ah, there's got to be nicer things to dwell on," he thought. "Oh yeah," he said to himself. "Last Monday was a lovely day when I revisited the Plaza Isabel la Católica."

It was on the Plaza Isabel that he and his family, totaling four, first lived so long ago in La Paz. In the apartment building that stood in those days next to the Hotel Crillon—today it is Hotel Ritz—they celebrated their first

Christmas in 1974. Those were frugal days, but they enjoyed having the last two of their five children at home. Those children were then 14 and 16 years old. Those youngsters went into the streets and breathed the air and returned home speaking Spanish. The mother and dad studied in classes all day and did homework half the night and couldn't do half as well as the children. His pride as a war veteran bristled as he sat in Spanish classes with German and Japanese youth, English speakers that studied Spanish in the same classes he did. He resolved tenaciously that those upstarts were not going to learn faster than he did. It was hard, but he determined to stay up. "Those aren't the most pleasant things to remember either," he thought.

A snack and soft drinks were served on the plane, and the break gave the older man a little reprieve from his wandering thoughts. That didn't last long, however, and anyway last Monday was such a pleasant day. As the plane was leaving behind some of the 2,500 miles of flight distance, he decided to dwell on the pleasantries of last Monday. He was there alone under the same ancient evergreen trees in Plaza Isabel. Even the concrete benches were the same and the statue of Isabel, the queen of Spain, looked exactly as she had 24 years earlier. By coincidence or design of the Lord, he found himself in the little park—the center of a huge intersection—during the midday's two-hour work stop. Truck drivers, construction laborers, gardeners, and others were lying on the grass napping in the warm sun. Children pulling cardboard and plastic toys on a string ran over the lush green grass shouting to each other. Students sat on the ground or concrete benches with their faces in books. An Indian woman, in typical dress, was breast-feeding her baby as she watched her older ones play.

One boy about 10 years old, with a colorful aguallo blanket draped across his shoulders, approached the old gentleman and played his harmonica. The aguallo portrayed the Christmas colors, and his harmonica tune was about the Virgin Mother and child. As soon as he stopped the music, he extended his hand for a coin. Had the man not been prepared with several small coins in his pocket, it would have been a small tragedy because other children were observing the hand out. Quickly he counted 10 children about him with smiles, asking in hushed voices for their coin as they extended empty hands. His camera was snapped to include them and a background of others before he would share his coins with them.

The man bought popsicles for three little girls from a vendor cart in the plaza and asked where they lived. The older of two of the children, who were sisters, said they were from Alto La Paz, fully nine miles from where they were standing. "How did you get here?" the man asked. "We walked," she replied. Whether the children wandered from home hoping to be entertained or be fed is anyone's guess. A youth named Elba stood in the plaza looking about for her mother, who was to meet her there. The man spoke to Elba intending only to make some friendly small talk. After the briefest of words he asked about the two dark growths on her face, and if a doctor had ever seen them. "They have been there all my life," she replied. "If they begin to itch, grow, or become sensitive, see a doctor," he said. Her mother showed up, and they smiled as they parted with an "hasta luego."

Time quickly passed as the 2 p.m. hour neared for the city to become alive and go back to work again. The adults began to leave the plaza to resume their activities of livelihood, and the man walked slowly toward his hotel a few blocks away. That was last Monday, but for the present he was flying higher than clouds, sitting between his wife and Mr. Pittman, immersed in his thoughts.

As the man on the airplane traveled away from Plaza Isabel on Avenida Arce in La Paz, crossing the equator into the winter-like Northern Hemisphere, his thoughts slowly and gently wandered on. He looked ahead in the third row ahead of them. On the same side of the big plane's aisle could be seen the top of a woman's head. Her hair alone was enough to distinguish her from being a Latin woman. She and her husband, who sat next to her, had also been registered in La Paz's Hotel Camino Real for the same number of days that the older traveler and wife had been there. That was exactly 10 days from arrival at and departure from La Paz. She and her husband were seen in the hotel's restaurant, the lobby, and taking taxis from and arriving back at the hotel. Their trip to La Paz was surely of a business nature for their dress generally was not what one would call casual. The old man and wife knew that woman and husband sitting up on the third row ahead of them. The woman was fully 48 years old and the mother of three daughters. The husband was of the second generation of Russian immigrant Jews that came to America at the turn of the century.

"What else could I say about that woman or remember that would be numbered among the pleasantries of our trip?" he thought. "She was the first of five children in her family, but who is he that would call that anything special? She began taking her first steps at 8 ½ months old, and playfully put on her mother's shoes as soon as she was walking well," his thoughts rambled on. "It's also a fact that as a young girl, she wanted to wear ladies' hose before her time and put on heels before it was pleasing to her father. She spent too much time on the phone with school friends and wanted to get her driver's license too soon." Ahhhh," the man nearly uttered audibly. "In the 48 years my wife and I have known that woman, what can be one of the most precious things to lend my thoughts to?" He mused quietly as the big Boeing jet, loaded to capacity, speeded across the Caribbean.

Travel fatigue was coming over the older man but sleep spurned his eyes. Mr. Pittman was napping and taking extra inches in his relaxed position. His wife, sitting on the right hand, was trying to relax and feigned to sleep some. The man turned his mind loose, as he peered at the back of the woman's head, but he held jealously to every thought. His mental pictures went faster than a computer back through the years to one mid-afternoon. It was on a lovely Sunday in the fall of 1951, in a relaxed family setting on the front porch of his parent's home. All was amiable, and the sun was invitingly warm. Some of the family present in the relaxed group included his parents, two brothers, their wives, and a baby just under 18 months old. That baby was the woman in the third row ahead on the big jet of American Airlines speeding northward to the U.S. Since that afternoon so long ago, the man's parents have moved on to eternity and his brothers have become grandparents. Regardless of what has happened since, the events of that yesteryear Sunday afternoon were engrossing enough to exclude all but the present. On that date, with its frightening activity, nothing would ever seem to be so important whether past or future.

Let it be said that the baby girl was the first grandchild to her paternal grandparents and was doted upon bountifully with all the affectionate attention grandparents can give. Being the only child in the group on that far off Sunday afternoon, she was never lacking an adoring gaze of one or more of them.

Without being noticed, and unimportant if it had been, someone gave the baby a piece of candy to suck on. The flavor was that of a common lemon drop. A little later with startled awakening, someone noticed that the child was struggling with something in her mouth or throat, and she was making some coughing efforts in a choking struggle. The mother grabbed the child up to open her mouth but nothing was visible; the candy had become lodged much deeper within her trachea. She was not breathing, and her body lurched with all her strength as she struggled for breath in her mother's arms. The warm pink in her face was fast becoming pale, and the mother became too emotional to remain rational. The time span only took seconds for the relaxed family setting to become startlingly aware and emotionally caught up in great alarm and then hysteria. Sensing absolute helplessness, the mother thrust the child into the father's arms who was none wiser and doubtfully stronger in that traumatizing moment. In anguish, she pleaded before God in a debilitating fear that overcame her quicker than tears.

The father, knowing little more than how to give battlefield morphine to a wounded soldier, abruptly grabbed the baby by the feet and began to shake her out as if she were a dust cloth. Unmindful of any other injury to her, he plunged her head downward even harder, adding an abrupt shake upward. Their little girl was motionless, pale in color, and unable to make a move or utter a sound. Others of the family began to beg and call upon the Lord for a miracle of restored life. For all practical purposes, she was undeniably dead. Trembling fear and agony forbade the man to be rational when he tried to retrieve the lodged candy by thrusting a finger deep in the child's mouth. He will never know if anything attempted in those seconds helped or worsened the tragedy, but he became nearly insane with emotion when he retrieved his finger with bloodstains on it.

Any doctor or hospital was too distant to be savior at that time, but something had to be tried. All that was attempted had proven futile to dislodge the candy, and the child lay limp and lifeless. The man's car was parked on the street in full view. Without plan or discussion, he grabbed the child with an impulsive move, tucked her under his arm as if she were a sack of cement, and jumped the two or three steps off the porch in an attempt to rush her to the hospital in his car. All hearts pleaded God's mercy, and all eyes forbade that anything happen without their detection. Landing on his feet soundly on the cement walkway, an appreciable elevation below the porch level of the house, something dislodged from the child's throat and bounced into view across the cement walkway. A hushed calm came over the scene, as they were afraid to believe what they had seen. As they all stood so tensed with fear and anxiety, one by one a feeling of thanksgiving and joy slowly began to come over each of them. They were all aware that their ability and wisdom had done nothing to restore that little girl to life. The God whom they served, and that loved them, had intervened wondrously and did easily and quickly what those parents, grandparents, and kinsmen couldn't do. The technique—now known as the Heimlich maneuver—may have unknowingly been applied, but it was God that worked the miracle.

For some moments, the child was hysterical with uncontrolled emotions. Whether the child's hysteria was from fear, pain, or both, no one cared. At that point, for all that had happened and transpired, the best doctor wouldn't have been able to provide the tiny girl's need like the arms and voice of its loving mother or the doting grandmother.

The high-flight memories were those of the retired elderly man who gazed at the back of the head of the traveling woman sitting just three rows ahead. They were flying in the clouds on an American Airlines Boeing 757 designated that day as flight 922, La Paz to Miami. Memories of what God had done for them as parents and a baby daughter nearly five decades before had strengthened his faith for the present and future. Furthermore, to be sitting next to the mother of that yesteryear baby was to him a tremendous comfort. On that American Airlines flight sat a 48-year-old mother, lovely and comfortably, who was that yesteryear baby. The elderly man thought, "These are good memories." Then he relaxed to take a nap.

Vondas A. Smith

The Little Earthquake

Written November 23, 1989

Prologue: A fish is never longer nor weighs any more by anyone's measure other than the man that caught it. An earthquake is also much more severe when told by the one that survived it. This is especially true if it were his first one to experience.

Sadnov and his family—totaling four—were in Lima, Peru, about six weeks after a particularly large tremor. It made havoc in the city that still had too many of the old-world adobe structures standing and in use. In that Pacific coast city of Peru, building with adobe, a large sun-baked dirt brick, is now forbidden in these more modern times. However, city ordinance or no city ordinance, there were adobe-built structures and an earthquake about six weeks before Thanksgiving Day, 1974.

One of the first things that Sadnov heard from the housewife of the host family was a recount of the quake and its great damage. Since he had never experienced one, at least not one severe enough to make teeth chatter, Sadnov hoped that their 10-day visit would pass without a quake.

"If you were to be awakened in the middle of the night with the whole world giving you the shakes, there will be no time for anything but to run out of the house. You pray that you can get out in time, and don't even pause to dress," she said. About two days and nights passed in total tranquility. Indeed he had about forgotten about the verbal scare, but it was filed away in his subconscious.

On about the third morning, well after daylight, Sadnov lay in his half-sized bed awake in the quiet of the morning. His son was sleeping in another small bed near by. In this serene setting, suddenly the invisible monstrous forces of nature, too independent to advise anyone, began to lurch and flex all its powers. Throughout the house, occupied by some 11 people, there was not a cry out from anyone. If it were Sadnov's youthful reflexes experiencing renewal or his well-programmed subconscious, whatever it was, he was immediately resurrected. In great strides, he was in his pants and racing out into the hallway.

In his super fast exit from the bedroom, he was fleeing shirtless and barefooted. He had left a bed that was shaking like gelatin and swinging like a hammock. For whatever reason he thought necessary, he had grabbed a shirt in hand as he sped down the hallway. At the end of the hallway stood the wife of the host family as calmly as a stump with a hand gesture saying as much as, "Just hold on." No one had to tell Sadnov that they had or were having an earthquake, so he didn't waste time compiling a question about what was happening.

There he stood before the madam of the house with his pants questionably secured, barefooted, and without his shirt on. There was no alternative except to wait and hear her advice. She calmly said, "Don't worry, go back to bed; it's just a small one."

Considerably humbled, he had no argument against one who knew her earthquakes. He was just happy that she did, and that he and his family had not visited them six weeks earlier.

~~~~~~~~~~~~~~~~~~~~~~~~~~~~~~~~~~~~

Vondas A. Smith

Mule Died in Zacatecus

Written August 1972

He sat discouraged, exhausted, and drained of all ability—even to include thinking. The man, his wife, and four children were quietly waiting to take a bus northward to Nuevo Laredo. The Mexican border town would give them entrance to Texas, fully another 200 miles away to the north. They wished desperately to be back in the U.S. where their native language would be understood. The not-so-clean surroundings of the large bus station were crowded and noisy. They were in Saltillo, Mexico, and it was a Saturday night in August 1972. Their auto accident insurance had expired at 3 p.m. on that afternoon, but not before killing a big mule hours earlier on the same day at 1:30 a.m.

The family had traveled over 400 miles since leaving Guadalajara, south of them, on the day before. After driving for hours on that Friday, tired and hungry, the family ate a lovely meal in a fine restaurant in Zacatecus. They had gotten a hotel room in that city on the way south to Guadalajara about a week before. Zacatecus is a lovely city at night, sitting high on a hill in the wasteland. It is called the air-conditioned city. This time while going north the family decided to make it only a rest stop, before starting again for an all night drive in the rain.

The time was 9:20 p.m., Saturday night, and Sadnov with his family sat numbly and unattached from all that went on about them. The last 20 hours had been an almost unbelievable experience. It was filled with horror, fright, and a sense of frustrating helplessness. The terrifying experience began at 1:30 a.m., when a full-grown, dying mule catapulted off the car leaving skin, hair, and a spray of blood.

There seemed to be a half dozen mules running wildly across the highway, but fortunately, only one in the middle was hit. The car continued upright only with the guiding hand and support of omnipotence. Though it is not known for sure, it is believed that the animal went over the top of the vehicle. There were no screams within the car, though one of them cried audibly: "Jesus, Jesus, Jesus." From another came a prayer in tongues as the wildly swerving car, traveling at 70 miles per hour in the rain, continued for a few hundred feet. The car hood bent upward in a blinding position and the motor stopped, leaving no power steering or brakes. When it came to rest on the lonely roadway, all seemed dead in the Zacatecus wilderness 65 miles from the nearest hamlet or gas station. The car sat in the cool night air in a cloud of steam as a traffic obstruction on a built-up roadway. Their fear had to be converted to calm reasoning, so they began to examine themselves for injuries. They found only minor bruises and a tiny scratch or two, so the first phase was over. The front of the car was demolished and sitting dangerously in the night blackness, partially blocking the roadway.

"What are we supposed to do, and what can we do?" he thought. The need for clearing the highway was an absolute necessity. Buses passed, but happily the first vehicle that stopped brought kind hands that could never be more appreciated. A government truck driver and his helpers towed the car and its six occupants through 65 miles of rolling hills and curves behind the big road tractor and trailer to the nearest city of Saltillo. The large truck threw an abundance of blinding road filth on the crippled car's windshield as they continued through the slow falling rain. As the towrope repeatedly broke and was tied again and again, it became increasingly more dangerous. After an unnerving two hours and twenty-five minutes, all was quiet again. The truck, driver, and helpers were gone, and the family of six sat numbly, waiting for the new day to dawn. The shreds of rope were still tied to the front of the car as they sat inside. They were parked on a muddy unpaved lot alongside a service station. The frustration and helplessness were felt immeasurably. There must be a police report, the insurance adjuster, family lodging, and transportation. These things in a land of strange laws and unknown people speaking a foreign language cannot easily be gotten without an interpreter. Not one member of the family could speak Spanish conversationally.

The Federal policeman that came to investigate was very irritated that the car had been moved from the scene of the accident. He pointedly noted that the insurance was invalid because of it. A preliminary report was made at 5 a.m., and Sadnov was told to report to the Federal Police Station at 10 a.m. The policeman also suggested that there would be a stiff fine. In the meantime, he would make the 65-mile drive south in search of the dead animal to verify the accident story. It is improbable that the policeman truly made that trip. After the police left, the family sadly watched as a government tow truck came to impound the car. A taxi was summoned to take them to a hotel where an English speaker could be found. This was another unplanned expense. Helplessness? Certainly, and it was coupled with increasing physical fatigue because it had been a day and a night since checking out of the hotel in Guadalajara.

While feeling the darkest side of the worse possible situation outside of death, something began to change about 9:30 a.m. on that Saturday morning. That was when the appointment was kept at the Federal Building, where Sadnov arrived a little early. The policeman said that the mule could not be found, but blood and tire marks verified our story. The insurance adjuster had a local office and was quickly summoned. He promptly took the police report, then he and Sadnov hurried to the police lot where pictures of the wrecked vehicle were made. A release document was arranged to transfer the wrecked vehicle to the custody of the insurance company on the following Monday. The automobile would be towed to the border town, Nuevo Laredo, to be repaired. All of this was quickly arranged before the Saturday noon closing hour. The insurance adjuster asked for a 20-peso tip to give the clerks for remaining a few minutes after their office's closing hour. Sadnov was in agreement because the hotel cost to remain in town for the weekend would have been 250 pesos a day. Paying 20 pesos to the clerks saved 500 pesos in hotel costs alone. There was no more talk of having to pay a fine. Sadnov was given permission to enter the police lot and remove all personal belongings from his car. A good meal and a little rest in the late afternoon made the waiting on Saturday night at the bus station much more pleasant.

Sadnov and his family sat in the Saltillo bus station that night with tickets and reservations for a five-hour bus trip to the U.S. border. The tangled events of the past 37 hours since leaving Guadalajara were more relegated to the past as each moment slipped by. A faint light began to appear at the end of their tunnel experience.

The family was exhausted in mind and body while awaiting the bus departure, and Sadnov sought the brighter side to relax and think about. He thought, "Yes, it was 9:20 p.m. a little while ago. The Federal Officer that investigated our accident saw the six of us here at the station. It was kind for him to come by to greet us one last time. He came alone, but then another officer approached and joined us. Seeing all six of us with our luggage, he came to exchange good-byes for one last time. His home was close to the bus station, and he had just returned from investigating another accident. He asked if I'd like to see the pictures of that accident. Of course I would, so he presented several photos, freshly developed, of the horrifying scene near town. Five died in one family, we were told. I wonder if it could be worse.

Well, I don't know, but they were on the way to a funeral, and now out of this there will be five more. Many things in life escape understanding and explanation. One thing for sure, when my problems become so big and my world so small, the Lord gives me more room to be able to cope with it."

"There's one other thing that puzzles me. Why does this Federal police officer keep coming into view? I haven't bought him off with any money for anything, and he's not asking for any. Could it be because my wife promised to pray for him to be able to find that mule? Whatever it is, he has become a friendly one to us. Anyway, we're happy now to leave that dead mule in the wasteland of Mexico's Zacatecus Province and go home with a pleasant memory of a kind policeman."

≈≈≈≈≈≈≈≈≈≈≈≈≈≈≈≈≈≈≈≈≈≈≈≈≈

The Miraculous Fuss

Written October 10, 1991

Maria was a 17-year-old Bolivian girl looking forward to her graduation from high school. The poverty of her family had never afforded vacations that many enjoy in today's world. Her mother died more than four years earlier, and she lived with her father and an older sister. The routine of her life, in spite of whatever ambitions she might have had, ranged from her home to school and to her church. Without doubt, her excitement was exceedingly great when a school trip was planned for about 40 girls in her graduation class. That trip would open to her and her classmates a whole world much greater than what they had ever known.

Leaving La Paz, the nation's capital city, the planned bus trip would take them to Santa Cruz, 16 hours away crossing two ranges of the Andean Mountains. It is the nation's second largest city and is much different due to its lower altitude and warmer climate. The group was well supervised by adult women teachers, and they were all ready to enjoy a weekend of activities.

Just as any girl her age, there was another girl that she considered her best friend. They began the trip sitting together and talking amiably as they rode over the level stretch of high plateau called the Altiplano. They were seated on the right side of the big bus. While they sat together talking during that first six-hour section of their long trip, one of them introduced into conversation a popular boy of the school that was known to them. For whatever reason, fatigue or conflict of common interest, they began to mix words and irritated one another. A rest stop was made in the city of Cochabamba, and the two girls decided to sit and chat with someone else. It happened that way as a mutual thing and continued as such during the rest of their trip.

After the group's enjoyable times together on the weekend in Santa Cruz, seeing the sights and loving it to its fullest, they were a great bunch of tired youths. Night came to end their Sunday, and within a few hours they were to begin the long return trip home. At the bus station they were anxious for the 10 p.m. departure time. It would afford comfortable seats and sleeping during the night as they passed the long hours over the monotonous roads of the lofty Andes.

Maria nor her girlfriend were quite ready to make up when they boarded the big bus of the Aroma Bus Line. Maria took a seat on the left side of the bus next to the window well behind the driver. Her girlfriend again took her place on the right side with another classmate. Very little time passed after the late departure hour before all was quiet and most were sleeping. At some time during that first four hours of the trip, the bus chauffeur turned his job over to his 17-year-old son. On board was a relief driver, but for reasons unknown, he was not at the controls.

The 2 a.m. Monday morning hour found the bus, loaded with high school girls and a few adult teachers, careening around the mountain curves. That roadway is one of the factors that help Bolivia maintain life expectancy at 51 years of age. Maria was asleep. She was seated next to the window while a sleeping classmate sat beside her by the aisle. Suddenly, there was an explosion that ripped apart their whole world. They found themselves being violently thrown in a death-dealing mixture of many bodies, luggage, glass, and bus seats. The direction of up ceased to be up, and down defied any direction. A tremendous veil of darkness engulfed Maria, and she could only cry out in the name of Jesus. Violently thrown from the roadway, the huge bus turned and rolled like so much junkyard debris down the mountainside. The mountain echoed with the screams and groans of the wounded and dying. Maria found herself miraculously mobile. She left her part of the wreckage by way of a window, but in her daze she returned to help whomever she could. She found the right side of the huge bus split open and lifted a seat from a classmate who had ceased to respond with signs of life. There were others. One student no longer had facial features to recognize. There were compound fractures and flesh torn from exposed bones of lower limbs. Two women teachers lay dead with some of their students.

Up on the roadway, at least two trucks stopped, giving hope that someone would help on the carnage-strewn mountainside in the cold night. The drivers descended the mountain to survey the scene of the bloody, dead, and suffering. Maria heard one man remark to another that it was a bunch of "collas." They returned to their trucks without lifting a hand. The word "collas" defined them as people of the high plateau, as opposed to the low-altitude people. Maria searched without a light in the night blackness for her friends. With bare hands she did what she could. She prayed, while eyes burned with tears, trying to encourage her friends until help could find them.

Maria recognized in the dark a hysterical girl, wounded grievously. She was her best girlfriend, and close by was the body of her seat companion. Identifying this body of her classmate was unmistakable. The mystifying workings of God are difficult to find answers to and many times are never known. Finding her girlfriend and a body nearby introduced a mystical question. How did Maria escape being the body of the girl who occupied the seat in which Maria once sat?

In the darkness of night among wreckage debris, down the mountainside from the road level, awaited the wounded with the dead. Those that could cry did, needing and hoping for their Samaritan to arrive. At the scene lay seven school girls and two teachers who would never again open school books. The childish fuss that Maria had with her girlfriend must have been the hand of omnipotence that reached out in the night to protect one Maria Soria.

The girl who occupied the seat that Maria had vacated was buried the next day, Tuesday, October 8.

Epilogue: Maria was the baby of five children born to Jaime Soria and his wife. She was much loved both in her family and church. Not known to Mr. Soria at that time was that another of his daughters would be lost in a similar mountain roadway accident a few years later.

Misfortune's Day Off

Written October 10, 1991

Misfortune has a perpetual holiday in many areas of the developing world, and Latin America is included in some of that. Crime, immorality, poverty, and ignorance are sometimes hidden beneath a canopy of religion, which rarely sees improvement from one generation to another. The experience of a young Christian girl named Angelica proves that hope does exist for individuals who will sincerely and faithfully serve God.

Angelica's father, Pedro, was fortunate to have had an income. It was sad that his work operating road-building equipment always kept him away from home. He grew tired of being separated from his family—often by great distances. His daughter, Angelica, was still at home after completing her high school years and helped with the younger brothers and sisters of the large family. They lived in the city of Oruro, a mining town high in the Andean Mountains of Bolivia, where the government had closed almost all the tin mining operation. There was no work whatsoever, and the family found themselves in dire circumstances.

Though Angelica had spent some time in La Paz with relatives during the previous year, she had returned to her home in Oruro with a great desire to help in a newly opened church mission in her city. She was well acquainted with the minister and others there, and they worked together in harmony. The inevitable came upon them as a family. Her father lost his job and became unemployed. Angelica had to leave home in hopes of supporting herself by finding a job. For her, it meant returning to La Paz where she still had church friends and an uncle with family.

A letter preceded her going to La Paz, which was addressed to the missionary's wife. The missionary woman, Sister Ruth, had lived nearly 17 years in La Paz and knew numbers of people in places where she shopped. There were the laundries, garment stores, grocery markets, beauty salons, money exchange houses, magazine stands, and a host of others that sometimes needed sales help. Fortunately, from among Sister Ruth's acquaintances, Angelica was called for an interview for a job. To give a verbal guarantee of Angelica's honesty and excellent Christian character, the missionary himself dressed in his finest to meet an appointment in support of Angelica.

She was given a job in a clothing store that had been closed for a time. The closure was caused by serious theft committed by previous employees. The job paid very little, but it was a start. Business was poor. After a few weeks, another young lady was hired. During one Monday morning, there just weren't any customers that were buying. A man with an accomplice did enter to do some browsing on that morning and looked, chatted, and stayed on for some time. They were given courteous attention and were being watched as closely as possible. At the end of the day, a check of all the displayed clothing and the few sales of the day showed that a $50 men's garment was missing. Despair fell upon all of them from manager to the two employees. This included Angelica who liked her job and was doing her best to be a good employee.

Early on Tuesday morning, Angelica was riding a city bus on her way to work. While passing through a downtown area, she noticed a policeman lifting a man from the sidewalk. Drunks often used the area in early mornings to sleep off their night's liquor. The bus passed slowly in the busy traffic just as the man was lifted to his feet. His face came into full view, and immediately Angelica knew the man's face.

Only the morning before, she had him and an accomplice under her watchful eyes to avoid losing any merchandise by theft in the store where she was still a new employee. It was so unlike the timid young lady that she was, but a great surge of boldness and courage possessed her. It was almost as if vengeance had consumed her. Immediately, she got off the bus and hastily approached the policeman to denounce the man as a suspect of the theft the day before. The policeman asked if she wanted him detained, and her ready reply was in the affirmative. His identity proved that he was not Bolivian, and during questioning it was learned that he had indeed stolen the garment that he was wearing and accused of taking from the store. He was anxious to pay for the theft, and an acquaintance of his was promptly called upon to do that.

In one stroke of God's blessing, Angelica became a veteran in sales, a trusted employee, and was presented a salary plan that gave her a percentage of her sales volume. Anyone knowing this little lady that started to work on a salary of $41.09 a month knows that the Lord whom she served did not overlook that humble one in a society where misfortune has a perpetual holiday.

~~~~~~~~~~~~~~~~~~~~~~~~~~~~~~~~~~~~~

Vondas A. Smith

Navajo Off His Reservation

Written October 16, 1973

Sadnov was so delighted about what he could do and did do. The dreaded specter, the phantom god of alcohol, never relinquishes its victims quickly or easily. This knowledge put a dull edge on his exuberance when he parted company with his short-time acquaintance in Salt Lake City.

At about 6:30 p.m. as Sadnov, with his wife and children, walked near the Salt Palace in Salt Lake City, his wife drew his attention to an Indian walking with them. Turning to spy the man, Sadnov engaged him in conversation. As quickly as that happened, the man asked for 50 cents. Sadnov wasn't mistaken when he accused him of having been drinking alcohol. There was no denial to that, and the Indian even told him what he had been drinking. Sadnov refused him the gift of 50 cents that the Indian said he needed for food. Sadnov bid his family to continue walking toward the hotel where they were registered guests, while he and the other man remained on the street engaged in conversation.

Sadnov spoke slowly and distinctly, sometimes repeating himself only using different words. He found also that he was asking the Indian to repeat himself some. The dear man's Navajo language posed a slight problem because his English was badly accented.

His trimmed black hair was uncombed. He appeared to have worn his warm clothes at least a few days. As they stood in a strange attachment together on the street in Salt Lake City, one could readily see that they had absolutely nothing in common. Jess Leftus had nowhere to go, Sadnov did. In an hour, the well-dressed Sadnov would be in church in the huge convention center of the city. Jess was hungry, but Sadnov had just eaten. Jess was lonely, but Sadnov, acquainted with so many of the convention people, was speaking to different ones as they passed by. He probably knew more people in Salt Lake City that night than he did in his hometown that he left two decades before. The only comfort for Jess was the seat in the bus station not far away, and his companions were the elements with wind being his god.

Jess Leftus was stealing Sadnov's time and asking for a handout. What Jess didn't know was that Sadnov was taking something from him also. It was known that Jess wanted money to get more liquor, but Sadnov took time for a little more subtle reason. At 58 years old, and alcohol worn, it would seem that the Navajo had less time to spare. If then they were wasting time, Sadnov was plainly beating the aging Navajo who, by reason of their ages, had less of it to lose.

Jess' mother on the reservation was 97 years old, and in a forlorn way, he said she must soon go home. His wife was also on the reservation, and his three children were married and had families. The nine or more grandchildren didn't know him well enough to care or could help if they did. Sadnov kept him talking, always about himself or something related to himself. Since he was so detached from all else on earth, and seemed to have done it all to himself, Sadnov reasoned that Jess' cause was the most important thing going to him. In the shortest timeframe imaginable, Jess had shown all his greatness and humility and began to indulge in some repetitions. At no time did Sadnov suspect that what he was hearing from the man was pure fabrications. He truly sounded like a man that was trying to reach out to something that would be genuine or someone that might be able to help him.

As they slowly walked and talked on the busy street, they crossed at the corner. In 100 yards or so they would be approaching a sandwich shop. The two were slowly walking and chatting, when suddenly in a surprised and shocked voice, Jess was unmistakably heard to say in a low voice, "I'm a lonely man."

Sadnov could not go farther without stopping. About some things, one can walk and talk, but what he felt at that moment to talk about couldn't be said as they walked. They stopped within sight of the sandwich shop about which nothing had yet been said. One of the reasons that he stopped was because he wanted to look into that Navajo's aging, dark face and at those unbelievably dark eyes. Sadnov thought, "I've captured an Indian, and I want to give him to the Captain of our Salvation."

Sadnov's heart beat fast as he told Jess of the Galilean who was often lonely and acquainted with sorrow and grief. The Bible does not speak of him ever smiling. These things, and finally his suffering and death, he accepted willingly and voluntarily. He bore these experiences so that in his resurrection, victory over death, he could be everyone's comfort and strength in such times. Loneliness and suffering are impermanent because Jesus makes it that way.

Sadnov was exuberant as he talked to a ready listener. He explained intelligently and in the simplest way the victorious life in Christ Jesus available to all. Through the life of this resurrected one, the Lord Jesus, no one ever needs to live in perpetual loneliness. Jess listened to the gospel message in its simplicity of faith, repentance, and Jesus name baptism. Sadnov wasn't finished talking, even though they had begun to walk again and entered the sandwich shop. He motioned Jess to a seat, and Sadnov sat beside him and ordered from the waitress what he wanted Jess to eat. In a few minutes, the waitress placed his meal before him. As Jess reached for a fork, he was restrained for a moment to hear that the right thing to do now was to make an expression of thanks before God. Sadnov briefly prayed asking God's blessing on the food, and the poor hungry man that was about to eat.

The small price paid to satisfy one Navajo's appetite was negligible, indeed, to what Jesus paid to solve that same Navajo's need. Jess got a testimony, a short sermon, and a meal, but Sadnov left richer. He reaped a satisfaction that for that day in 1973, he had done what Jesus would have wanted him to do.

~~~~~~~~~~~~~~~~~~~~~~~~~~~~~~~~

Vondas A. Smith

Big-Headed Wisdom

Written October 10, 1989

On the first day of January during the roaring '20s, a boy was born in a small Mexican town named Guamuchil. He grew up to be a lover of books. Education was more than a dream; he pursued it. After his high school graduation, and having personally taught himself English for three years, he received a scholarship to study theology in a U.S. bible college. One day the boy named Manuel told his college roommate about his experience in once trying to buy a hat.

Buying a hat wasn't such a big task back when most men wore them. It was somewhat difficult for Manuel, however, simply because his head called for a size 8 ½.. While browsing in a hat department of a store one day, Manuel found what he was looking for. He tried it on, and it felt right on his head. He went to a mirror, and he also liked the way it looked on his head.

He decided to buy the hat, but one thing was lacking. It did not have a price tag on it. That could easily be learned from a helpful salesman, so he asked the price. "This one sells for $10," replied the courteous salesman. Manuel had hoped that it would be within his buying range, but he simply did not have the $10. Furthermore, it was an excessive price for a hat during that time, even for one of value such as he chose.

Manuel wanted the hat seriously enough to present a bargain that naturally stated the matter in his own favor. "Look," he said, "this has to be an overstatement in the price. Hats of this quality generally sell for less." Now a good salesman has to have ready-made answers to tear away at any opposition to a purchase that any would-be buyer might make. This man was a good salesman.

"Let me tell you, sir, you can not find a good hat just anytime that will fit your head," spoke the salesman. "You wear an extra large size, and I suggest that you buy this. It has real quality." Without much hesitation, Manuel gave his own reply to the salesman's wisdom. "If you think it is hard for me to find a hat to fit my head, you should try to find a head to fit this hat. You see, sir, you have the same difficulty that I have."

Vondas A. Smith

Irene's Lard Bucket

Written November 16, 1989

Irene was the only daughter of four children. As a child at home with three brothers, she found no competition to her opinions and demands, so it was completely normal for her to grow up to be just a little domineering. If Irene wasn't perfect as a wife and mother, then it was only because she was human.

She married Billie, who was one of eight children, while both of them were still teenagers. Sometime during the decade of the '30s that became known as the "great depression," Billie acquired a taste for alcohol. However, it wasn't necessarily the hard times of those days that brought Billie to the bottle. He followed his dad who also was a lover of the bottle's escape.

There was a day when Irene's father-in-law was charged with public drunkenness and landed in the city jail for a weekend of merry-making. Billie visited his dad in jail to find that he was not fond of the jailhouse rations. "I'll tell Irene to fix you up a lunch," Billie told his dad. That was the end of the matter, and the lunch was to be for the following day.

During those times, the housewife's cooking fat was either pork lard or butter. Pork lard was commonly sold in metal buckets, and the buckets were useful for lots of things. No one ever threw away a lard bucket as long as it was considered a good one. It was not uncommon to have one or more on hand around the kitchen. It was convenient to use the bucket for packing lunches, and this is exactly what Irene did for her father-in-law. The lunch pail, as it was commonly called, was prepared and placed conveniently to await Irene's trip downtown. Her walk to the city jail was scheduled to be the first thing after lunch that day.

After the noon meal, with Irene ready for her walk to the city jail, she passed through the kitchen, picked up the lunch pail, and left. It was a hot afternoon to make a 30-minute hike to the jail with her father-in-law's lunch bucket. However, she made the errand as if it were routine, left the lunch pail with the jailer, and made her exit to the street to return home.

The jailer accepted the bucket from Irene to be given to her father-in-law. In his usual precautionary manner, he opened it for a simple inspection to make sure it contained no weapon. That was when the jailer hastened out to the street, with bucket in hand, to catch Irene and ask a question. "Lady, are you sure that you wanted to leave this bucket of lard for that man?"

~~~~~~~~~~~~~~~~~~~~~~~~~~~~~~~~~~~~~~~

Great Ant Fighter

Written September 23, 1989, La Paz, Bolivia

For anyone to say that he didn't like Ricardo is simply to say he didn't know him. On the other hand, just about anyone would say that he wasn't orthodox in much of anything. His study and reading never seemed to include Shakespeare, but no one would dare call him a dummy. Ricardo was different from Einstein, however, in that he combed his hair and didn't make atomic bombs. He was too young for the Selective Service System to grab him up for World War II, so he shifted from the defense factories of Michigan and the motherland down in Arkansas. Somewhere in his moving about in those two extremes, he came upon a philosophy of "mind over matter." For a time, it nearly became a religion to him.

One day in a jovial mood, partially back-slidden from his newly embraced doctrine, Ricardo told about one of his venerable mind-ascending, material-smashing experiences. A common species of the little house and garden ant had invaded his kitchen. He found himself at home alone, so he tried to figure out how to handle the situation. There was definitely a solution; he only had to set his thinking into action.

In his well-furnished modern home, well stocked with every necessity to make life comfortable, there was no way that the tiny ant could disrupt as brazenly as they had and survive. In a practitioner's way, he tried one simple remedy and then another. Nothing was repelling the tiny savages, and they were covering everything. Ricardo was too macho to be doing the stack of dishes that needed washing, but "mind over matter" would work. In his survey of any available weapon on hand, he spied a bottle of Clorox-like substance. It possibly could have been just that, and he began to give the unwanted multitude of ants great doses that speedily sent them off to eternity.

He was one delighted man of worthy accomplishment, seeing that he had come upon such a history-making discovery. There was no doubt that the unwanted ants were forever repelled. As Ricardo was finishing the recount of his experience, a smile began to gleam through his mustache. The ants truly died, but the tarnish to the silverware in the sink hardly seemed to make it all worthwhile.

~~~~~~~~~~~~~~~~~~~~~~~~~~~~~~~~~~~~~~

Vondas A. Smith

Crab-Infested Waters

Written October 14, 1989

Three children were taken from their surroundings in the country with its open spaces of fields and pastures simply because their dad got a job in the city and moved there. Living in town didn't take away their love for the country. Since many of their relatives continued living on the farm, there were always welcomed opportunities to visit the farm again.

During the summer vacations from school classes, plans were always made to visit Uncle Jim's farm. There were animals, and there were rain-filled stock ponds to supply the drinking water. One summer before a visit to the farm for a few days, one of the three brothers made plans for a boat trip across the waters. He planned his boat and began work on it. Being short on experience and expertise in boat building, his boat construction was a complete disaster. By the time the boat was placed in the water, the water was in it.

Those children's minds occupied them in as many ways as humming birds can fly. If they couldn't sail the waters, then they would swim the waters. There were two ponds for them to conquer. Now that particular summer was a dry one, and the water level in the ponds was low. Deep water presented them with no problem, but there was some deep mud on the bottoms of the ponds. Six racing feet stirred the water and mud until the frogs vacated their habitat.

Now Uncle Jim was presented with a worse problem than that of too little water for the stock. What he had left became too muddy for the cattle to drink. Uncle Jim's visiting nephews belonged to his only sister, and he wasn't about to reprimand them, but something had to be done.

In the city about six miles away at the Home Ice Company, the uncle had also gotten a job as an ice deliveryman to residences. That company had modernized from the old ice wagons and stepped up in the modern world, making ice deliveries by truck. Uncle Jim was a driver and had a regular job. He commuted to work in his own Model A Ford every day.

It is completely unknown how deep sea crabs came to town alive, but there were some that fell into possession of the ice company where Uncle Jim worked. To see one of those crabs was a first for more than a few people. That beastly thing of the sea with the spider appearance didn't invite anyone's casual touch. Just the sight of it from its peers was enough, and that glimpse was preferably made at arm's length.

With a live crab, Uncle Jim had the solution to the muddy water-loving nephews. Late one afternoon, the Model A arrived from town. Out stepped the favored uncle with two large cans in hand. Curious eyes of all the family plus three nephews viewed for their first time such a creature from the deep. His investment only bought one crab, but he had two buckets or large cans.

To his nephews, the ferocious crab was well documented by the uncle to be most dangerous. Uncle Jim explained his mission, and then he invited them to accompany him to the pond where he planned to raise them to sell commercially. Curious eyes from the three boys never missed a thing. They saw him fill the can that contained the crab until it was full. He then began to pour water into the empty can and dip it into the muddy pond. Each can was dipped into the filthy pond, both filling it and partially pouring it out again. Having two ponds about a hundred yards apart, he went to the second and repeated the ritual.

In the end nobody, not even the uncle, knew which pond was going to be supplying the county with all the crabmeat they would ever be buying. It is certain that the crab farm venture was a failure, but from that day forward the cows and horses had plenty to drink. If the pond water wasn't crystal clear, it wasn't chargeable to the vacation pleasures of three nephews.

~~~~~~~~~~~~~~~~~~~~~~~~~~~~~~~~~~

Accidents, Gals, and Camera

Written November 20, 1989

Prologue: Some have said that beauty lies in the eyes of the beholder. It might also be said that innocence or guilt of the same right or wrong could be viewed differently, depending on who did it.

An accident victim lay recovering in an Army hospital in a large U.S. city. Next to him, in the corner of the hospital ward, lay a motorcycle policeman recovering from polio. He would be left handicapped and unable to continue his outside job, but he would later return to work in Memphis in the state driver's license bureau. We shall call his name Stone.

Down at the opposite end of the hospital ward, there was a U.S. armed service veteran who had been convicted of armed robbery. While he was serving his sentence in prison, he had suffered a fall while working at the prison that left him with a permanent handicap; however, he was mobile in a wheelchair. The state trooper would never ride a motorcycle again, and the convict would suffer a lifetime handicap. Each of the two men, with a background of having been on opposite sides of the law, would have to look forward to a future with a different lifestyle.

Farley, the convict, was mobile in his wheelchair, but Stone, the policeman, was a bed patient alongside the other accident victim who was witness to what went on between those two men. Farley, for fun or mischief, would not agree with anyone about anything, especially Stone, the policeman. That participating witness to what went on between Farley and Stone viewed Farley's attitude and mannerisms for weeks. The onlooker would say that Farley earned a reputation of being just plain ornery.

One episode of the verbal head banging between them took place a day or so after Stone's wife and twins visited him on a Sunday afternoon. It was a beautiful spring afternoon about the first of May. Stone's wife and children arrived for their visit together and she brought, according to his instructions, an impressive case filled with some very fine camera equipment. He had obviously invested plenty, probably not very long before his polio attack. He had it spread across his bed checking it, and of course, admiring his fine equipment.

Farley, being mobile in his wheelchair, had missed nothing during the Stone family's Sunday afternoon visit together. Farley observed the impressive array of the expensive camera and related equipment with keen surveillance. He wheeled by Stone's bed later and opened a conversation about the camera. Stone was open and talked freely. "Why have you invested so much money in a hobby of photography, since photography couldn't possibly be the business of a state trooper?" asked Farley. "When I investigate accidents, sometimes I take pictures," responded Stone. "What do you do with the pictures?" questioned Farley. "I just sell them to someone—victims, reporters, a lawyer—to whoever has the best price," he said. Farley had something to think about as he left and wheeled down the corridor of the hospital.

Coming back down the aisle in his wheelchair sometime later, Farley wheeled up to the corner bed of the hospital ward to address Stone. "I've decided how I can make a good living when I get out of here," he said. "What do you plan to do out there in the world this time," asked Stone. "I'm going to get me an outfit like your photography stuff, get two or three lovely girls, and go to Florida. There we'll stake out a convention center frequented by big executives, and the girls will arrange dates with the businessmen away from home. All I plan to do is take pictures and sell them to the men or send them to their wives," said Farley.

Stone was not speaking in gentle tones when he told Farley, "I see that you may as well get ready to go back to prison." "Why would you say that?" Farley asked. "What would be the difference in me selling pictures and you selling pictures?" he questioned. "How could yours be right and mine be wrong? We would both be in the same business."

~~~~~~~~~~~~~~~~~~~~~~~~~~~~~~~~~~~~~~

Vondas A. Smith

Girl's Facial and Boy's Piano

Written December 7, 1989

As a teen-aged girl, RaNae was as lovely as any girl to be found, but like most girls she always sought to improve on her good looks. When she was still very small, she was found to have a severe sight problem, and her corrective lenses were as much a part of her as her name. RaNae did her face and hair preparations for bed one night and retired to bed in her usual manner.

At some very late hour while all were asleep, she and the rest of the family were awakened with some especially loud knocking at the door. Her father answered to find a uniformed police officer that calmly told him about an accident out on their front lawn. Other members of the family, in robes or pajamas, quickly joined the two at the front door, and everyone except RaNae accompanied the police officer across the lawn to view the scene of the accident.

A lovely cottonwood tree in the corner of the front lawn was no longer standing. A big black Oldsmobile occupied the place of the tree, with ample damage to its front. The tree was protruding from beneath the auto both in front and rearward. Some of the neighbors were awakened, and at least one joined the police and the family group that had suffered the loss of their tree. He was Bobby, the piano-playing boy, who lived across the street.

RaNae had eyes for Bobby and at least some thought that perhaps Bobby also had eyes for RaNae. It was RaNae who was the last to join the scene, and she was completely uninformed about what happened. She was full of questions about the scene since she was unable to see well.

RaNae, standing on the lawn in the darkness, was dressed in a house robe and not wearing glasses. Her long hair was made into a mammoth stack on her head, curled around large hard-paper rollers. Those rollers are known by everyone to be the throw-a-way items of a common paper product that is familiar in every home. The cosmetic mask that covered RaNae's face was colored an unforgettable hue of Halloween green. All of this was meant to make her beautiful for the next day.

Knowing where she was and recognizing the voices of all her family, she sought to be informed about what had happened. One responded by saying, "Aww, some drunken driver or sleeping driver ran off the street and knocked our tree down. He got out and left his car."

With good intentions and wanting only to be helpful, Bobby added his voice to the conversation. At hearing Bobby's voice, RaNae was smitten with embarrassment too great to be measured. Learning that he was present, and able to see her face and hair made up as it was, came as a shock that knew no rational response. There was nothing that she could do that would have added dignity to the occasion. She was caught outside with an unforgettable green face, and her head made mammoth with her long hair wound on huge hard-paper rollers.

Dejectedly, she began to move back toward the house. With all the trauma of a profound teen-aged crisis, she envisioned nothing less than the end. A romance was in the making, but it ended so abruptly. "How could he have dared to invade my privacy by coming at such a time?" she thought.

It isn't unreasonable to imagine what Bobby was thinking as he returned across the street. "I guess I'll never understand girls. RaNae was so rude she wouldn't even speak. With a cold shoulder she told me off without even opening her mouth."

Bobby returned to his piano practice each afternoon, and as usual the cords of music drifted across the street. Each night RaNae did her face and hair in her usual manner in preparation for the next day. No one will ever know if the Oldsmobile that killed the cottonwood tree also killed something even lovelier that could have happened in the lives of RaNae and Bobby.

Epilogue: From that summer night in Memphis when the Oldsmobile climbed the cottonwood tree, it was impossible to envision that a 27-year marriage would dissolve for RaNae later in life. It is hoped that Bobby's adult years were filled with more durable benefits, blessings, and pleasantries in his own married life.

≈≈≈≈≈≈≈≈≈≈≈≈≈≈≈≈≈≈≈≈≈≈≈≈

Answering a Silly Question

Written September 26, 1989, La Paz, Bolivia

In the early 1950s, when railroads were in a mad rush to dispose themselves of the last vestiges of the steam locomotive era and their labor unions were bargaining for a five-day work week, some jobs were created. Railroads needed some tough men to cope with the outside work, the night hours, and their hard-driving supervision. It was during such a time that some tough young men, with families to provide for, came out of the woods of neighboring states to the big city of Memphis. The old Frisco Railroad was no exception during those days of needing some good men. Up from a farm in Mississippi came a slow-talking, tall man with a young family. He needed work, and the Frisco Railroad needed a man who wanted to work. He never seemed to pick up a nickname like so many others. There were those who were known as Moo Cow Moore, Hog Jaw Campbell, Meat Head Boyd, Doe se Doe Walker, Cedar Leg Rockholt, and on and on. These were real men, and no less than the farmer from Mississippi who was always called by his real name, Furtick.

It may be said that Mr. Furtick had his own ambitions and dreams of financial independence. It was his misfortune to be injured once on the job, and some of the fellow employees began to think he intended to use that leverage to retire. It didn't work out that way, however. He was a grand enterprising thinker, and he was seldom jovial about anything. One day on the job, he was in serious conversation with some of his co-workers, and he told them about the exploration that an oil company had begun on his farm back home. The drilling rig was hard at work already.

Mr. Furtick was one of those most unusual men that had no extreme to his emotions. He was a low-key man, a ready talker, and easy to be with.

109

Most of those that knew him in his newly adopted environment of the big city did not have the full measure of discernment to know when Mr. Furtick was telling it straight or simply hallucinating. It's true that his oil rig story didn't enjoy a great following of faithful believers. Indeed a few began to joke about it, but in an undercover manner, because no one wanted to provoke the ire of that straight-faced, tall man from Mississippi.

One day some of his fellow workers were asking about the drilling rig's progress and the prognosis of his coming riches. That was the day that Mr. Furtick told his co-workers about the rig's great ease in reaching an immense depth into the earth. Nothing seemed to impede the rig's advance. There was one small curiosity that the drilling crew encountered, however, at about 10,000 feet below. Anxious ears were ready to hear the rest of the story, and truly his buddies were imploring for more. Mr. Furtick paused only for a contemplative second when he slowly began again. "At about 10,000 feet into the earth, the drill bit smashed into an old Cyprus tree stump," said Furtick. Unbelieving such a fabrication, one of the men asked, "Now tell us, Furtick, how was it known to have been a Cyprus tree stump?" Furtick replied, "Well, they took a sample of the stump water to a laboratory, and the analyses proved it had been an old Cyprus tree."

A Chipmunk's Weekend

Written October 30, 1989

Saturday afternoon, Jason and Logan were given the task of washing the green Chevy. Since it was the better of two relatively old cars, the boys' parents thought they should at least drive a clean one to church on Sunday. The boys were outside doing the job when they saw Alvie, the cat, chasing a little chipmunk. Alvie loved to pester and antagonize the little creatures that he eventually ate. Alvie was running around the car and getting in the boys' way. Then Jason, feeling sorry for the chipmunk, got a tree twig and put it down in front of the chipmunk to save him. The chipmunk, hastening to take advantage of the stroke of good luck, ran up the twig and continued up Jason's arm to finally perch on his shoulder. The chipmunk seemed to have decided that Jason was the lesser of the two evils. Jason was quite delighted and brought him into the house to show the rest of the family.

The chipmunk did not seem to be in any hurry to leave Jason, so the proud owner of the new pet proceeded to carry him on his shoulder for most of the afternoon. Jason's mother finally became wary of the chipmunk jumping off, so she put him in an old parrot's cage. Little did she realize that this was just the beginning of trouble. The boys, together with their mother, played with the little creature off and on all afternoon. He would let them pet him, and he accepted food right out of their hands. They fed him peanuts and sunflower seeds, and he seemed quite content. But then the family left about 6:30 p.m. that evening to go to a Halloween party and hayride at the church in Tishomingo, Mississippi. When they got home that night about 11 p.m., the cage was empty. The boys were heartbroken because Henry, the chipmunk, was gone.

He obviously decided it was no longer fun to be in the cage with no one to play with, and being so little, he probably just went through the bars of the cage. The children's mother did not sleep well that Saturday night with the chipmunk lost in the house. She could just imagine waking up to a small creature scurrying all over her bed. The family was gone from home nearly all day Sunday, but during the short time that they were there, they searched for Henry to no avail.

Monday morning dawns, and the clock alarm goes off at 5:45 a.m. Time to get up and get the children out of bed. Karisha, the daughter, was a sleepy head because she spent all weekend in Tishomingo, which included a Friday night slumber party, a Saturday night Halloween party, and Sunday activities in church. Since the mother did not make the children's school lunches on Sunday afternoon as usual, she went into the kitchen about 7 a.m. Monday to do that little chore. But, look! ... The first signs that a chipmunk was loose in the house were obvious in the kitchen. He had found the loaf of bread.

Their last loaf of bread looked like a mouse had been eating on it, and there were little crumbs everywhere. By that she knew they had this little animal around, alive, and well. Since this was their last loaf of bread, she needed to see if any of it could be saved. She reached into the loaf of bread and pulled out four or five slices of the bread. They looked all right, but still it gave her a queasy nasty feeling to think about it. She wouldn't have wanted to eat a sandwich made with that bread. She reached into the loaf to pull out a few more of the slices. As she reached into the loaf the second time, her fingers touched a "foreign object." At that same instant, the chipmunk leaped out of the loaf of bread with such force that he landed on her breast, ran up to her shoulder, jumped to the floor, scurried around, and went behind the breakfast bar on which the microwave was sitting. The mother was making so much hysterical noise that Jason ran into the kitchen and pleaded to know if his mother was all right. Although the mother can never move that bar to clean behind it, her adrenaline was flowing so freely that she reached over and just pulled the bar out. Later, when the chase was over, she could not push it back in place again without some help.

With the mother and three children grabbing at Henry, the chipmunk, he escaped from the kitchen into the dining room, made a pass through the den, scurried down the hall, and entered Karisha's bedroom. The mother would have never been able to chase a mouse that way. Since she knew Henry was a cute little chipmunk, albeit a potential big problem, she helped in the fast chase. Now the boys had new beds, box springs and mattresses, which were bought for them for Christmas by their grandmother. Since chipmunks like to burrow holes into the ground, they were afraid Henry might do that to their living room furniture or mattresses. For this reason, they immediately closed Karisha's bedroom door, called the dad from his morning shower, and brought in Alvie, the cat, from the outside. Surely, they thought, with all six of them in one room to chase little Henry, they could catch him in no time.

It took about 35 minutes to catch little Henry. The children were late for school, and the mother was late for work. Alvie, the cat, was absolutely no help. He must not have been hungry. That lazy cat was lying down by the door as if he hoped they would open it and let him out of that "mad" room. During the chase in the bedroom every piece of furniture was pulled out into the center of the room, which also included dismantling Karisha's bed. In the end, the little rodent crawled into a cardboard tube, which a poster paper had come in. The mother placed her hands over both ends of the tube and with shivers going up and down her back; she rushed to the back door. In one quick release, Henry was again out on the patio from which he had escaped the cat on the previous Saturday. Henry, like the dummy he appeared to be, just sat there on the patio. That was when Alvie, the cat, came alive again and immediately began chasing Henry all over.

The boys, Jason and Logan, sent up cries of alarm, but for one mother, the dear little Henry had had his chance. She certainly couldn't make any plans to interfere with his fate again because her nerves couldn't stand it.

Even today she has a hard time sticking her hand into a loaf of bread since Henry spent the weekend with them. She hopes to be able to recover from those fearful memories. The best of all the benefits from the chipmunk visit is that the kitchen got a good scrubbing on that Monday night.

~~~~~~~~~~~~~~~~~~~~~~~~~~~~~~~~

My Carlew Lost His Health

Written November 29, 1989

His railroad buddies always affectionately addressed M. Y. Carlew as My Carlew. His initials were as such, and leave it to a railroader to figure out what to do with that. He was not an imposing big man, but he had the energy and personal drive of one much bigger. In the city of Memphis, he was never content with one occupational job. He had his railroad occupation, and he also worked as a spray painter in an agricultural machine manufacturing plant.

Before he moved to Memphis from his small community in Arkansas, My Carlew worked as a pilot for an agricultural crop-dusting business. That work is altogether seasonal, but when there is work, the pay is said to be exceptionally very good. Being a young man with a growing family, and a seasonal occupation giving him time on hand, he decided to move to Memphis and find a more stable occupation. He did, and one of his occupations was a switchman job for the old S.L.S.F. "Frisco" Railroad. Being the likable and pleasant man that he was, he became everyone's friend.

One day, while on his railroad job, My Carlew's crop duster flying days became a topic of conversation. He talked freely about his experiences, why he trained for that work, and the whole matter was thoroughly discussed. While talking about those "stunt flying days" as a duster pilot, he made it sound adventuresome.

One of the men on his railroad crew must have been a little mercenary minded when he posed a question to My Carlew. "If you were making that kind of money, why on earth did you come to this railroad to labor out the rest of your life?" he asked. "I have the answer to that question," said My Carlew.

My Carlew went on to relate how the business in his part of the country was becoming a bit competitive. The farmers were often times wanting an aerial show as much as they wanted poison dust spread across their fields. As a time-saving measure, often there would be only an interview with the property owner, for as a local pilot he had general knowledge of everyone's farm in the county. "What is the acreage and the length of the field to be sprayed or dusted?" would be the starter question. This may or may not be done by phone, but more often than not, there would be no on-site inspection.

From descriptive conversation, a chart would be made. It would include the size of the field or fields, the location, type of spray to be used, how much cost, and the date and time would be set. As a last matter, but a very important one, the safety question would be presented. "Now tell me, sir, how tall are the trees around the property and where are they located?" My Carlew would ask. "There are no obstructions whatsoever," the farmer replies. "Well and good, that simplifies the work and cuts the time," My Carlew answers.

Early on the appointed morning with his plane ready to fly and loaded to an absolute capacity, he struggles to get it airborne. Once his plane is in the air, there is a sense of relief by having his heavy load airborne and ready to start dumping. With sure direction, he heads to his destination like a migrating goose. He doesn't need to inspect anything for that has already been covered. With a trained eye, experienced hand and feet, and his computer-like brain measuring time, distance, wind factor, weight, speed, and perhaps a dozen other things, he has started to survive the danger of another day.

He bears down on his target like a fighter pilot and surely enough, everything is wide open. He begins to think he could eat his lunch and never miss a pass while doing a job as simple as this. To make the farmer happy, and be sure that he is surveying from some vantage point, My Carlew would be knocking blossoms out of the cotton stalks. A few feet higher would actually be better for it would give a more uniform coverage of poison on the crop, but it is good business to please the farmer.

He is content to start dumping for this begins to lighten his payload. After those brief seconds of the first run he is ready to pull up and away from the ground. As if he were hit by lightening, his whole being is charged with an indescribable bolt. To merely call it a shock would be a gross understatement. With struggling hands and feet and a prayerful heart, he impulsively labors to miss the high-tension power lines before him. With nerves tempered like steel, his whole person struggles at the controls and with the plane's hard-laboring engine they miss the death-dealing electrical wires by mere inches. My Carlew is so relieved with the escape that he immediately falls back into his work schedule as if that death trap were part of the action.

"The work is interesting," said My Carlew. "Too frequently you hear about others that go to work and never get the job done, and some die trying," he said. "I've finished jobs without a thought or memory of anything that might have been life threatening," he continued. "All goes well until you're peacefully sleeping at home with your wife some night, maybe two or three weeks later. All of a sudden, some night in your quiet sleep, you run into a death trap of high-tension electrical cables or some other structure. With one short scream, your wife goes flying across the room to the floor and with hands welded to the head of the bed you wake up still kicking your way to safety."

"So you ask me why I left the high-paying job?" he questioned. He then added, "I'll tell you. My health failed me when a big yellow streak of fear began growing down my back."

Stormy Dog, the Ghost-Eater

Written October 7, 1989

A family of seven arriving at home parked their car in the driveway one rainy night. The children as one all spilled out of the car as only four sisters and a brother would know how to do. With their light hearts and chatty mood, it became a scramble as each wanted to be the first into the house. As quickly as the door was unlocked, the children scampered inside.

Before their dad had locked up, and as quickly as feet can move children, two frightened girls were back at the front door to announce that someone was in their bedroom. A horrifying hush fell on all of them.

"Did you see anyone?" whispered the dad. "No, Dad, but when I started to open the door, it moved," replied one daughter. He looked at another daughter who shared the same bedroom and asked, "Did you see it move?" "Yes, Daddy, I did," was the reply.

It was evident that someone was in the room. They all looked to him for answers, and for a frightful minute there were none. After a moment's thought, with a whisper they were told to remain in the living room and chat as normally as possible. The dad would go past that bedroom door to the den and get a rifle. This was done. They were then told with a whisper to make as much noise as they normally would by leaving the house. They were all to leave, close the front door of the house, get in the car, and drive away.

When they were all gone, there were at least two people left in the house, and one had a rifle. The battle of nerves was on. The dad of the family took a reclining position on the living room carpet with rifle at the ready. He looked down the hallway in the dark at the bedroom door that moved when the two daughters were prepared to enter the room. It was time for bed, but the tired family became occupied in a standoff crisis. The silence that reigned in the house occupied by two couldn't have been greater. Each awaited the other.

Time passed slowly, and the minutes seemed to be hours. One man was prepared to kill, and he hoped that the other was prepared to die. The dad was prepared to claim rights allowing him to shed the blood of an intruder into the sanctity of his private home. His eyes became accustomed to the dark. The dad was not a stranger to his rifle. Even in the house he had playfully fired shots into the rustic log fireplace mantle on several occasions. Now, for the first time in his life, he was waiting to shoot, if necessary, a human.

The dad's nerves became even more tensed as time passed slowly. The intruder was either comfortable enough to go to sleep or scared enough not to make a sound. It had been raining outside, and though it had stopped, the outside world was wet. While doing his best to hold on to his sanity in this battle of nerves, the dad suddenly heard the faintest sound possible at a side door to the house. That door was no more than five feet from where he was laying on the carpet. His sharp eye in the dark was immediately focused on that door to his right, and unbelievingly, he could see the doorknob turn.

The crisis had suddenly become critical. One intruder was in the house and now another, possibly his lookout, was entering. The rifle was trained on the second door before it began to open. There was no face or voice and his nervous finger was prepared to pull the trigger and blast a hole through the door.

The door was slowly opening, and he knew absolutely that he was not hallucinating. He would have wanted it that way had he been given a choice. Enough adrenaline was pouring into his blood to provide enough for a company of fighting men. Just before a face was given to the body behind the door, a very, very hushed voice was heard, "Shhhhh, Daddy, it's me."

His emotions immediately took more changes of direction than there are colors to the rainbow. How could he become angry, but how could he be calm? Seeing that for more than 20 minutes he had been prepared to shoot anything that moved in the house? That lovely daughter, about 13 years old, had probably come closer to death than either of them will ever know.

She was directed to sit on the floor to join in with her dad's vigil in the night. Not long afterwards, the family car was heard returning to the driveway. After entering the house, all again went into a crisis meeting to decide the next move. The facts were gone over again exactly as it happened when they initially entered the house. In this, nothing had changed, but enough time had gone by to leave place for questions. Those questions needed an answer by some means other than lying on the carpet all night with a loaded rifle trained on a bedroom door.

The family dog, a great guard dog, was a mixed collie and shepherd named Stormy. It was a stormy night when she was first brought home as a pup. She never was trained to be a housedog, and it was no small matter to persuade the wet dog to come into the house. The big dog was picked up bodily and carried into the house. Down the hallway, and like lightening, the dog was thrown into the room. The door was slammed, and the dad jumped aside from the door to hear a fight inside.

The scuffle was only minimal. But there was a bit of noise. After being convinced that Stormy was holding captive a real, live intruder in their home, the confident family was all emboldened to make their inspection without paralyzing fear.

With caution, they slowly opened the door. Seven pairs of eyes belonging to parents and children peered into the room. They expected to behold the ghastly figure of a huddled burglar cowered beneath the watchful eye of a mean dog, Stormy.

In the silence of the night, as no one breathed, they were confronted with a big wet dog contentedly relaxing comfortably on a once clean bed. That scene indelibly imprinted itself in the minds of that frightened family as they returned to their playful and chatty mood.

They retired for the night, happily calling out in the dark to one another from bedroom to bedroom in their customary way. "Good night, sleep tight, I love you," were the exchanges, repeatedly made. In place of a tragedy in that bedroom, it had fled the peaceful home twice in the same night. All were happy and grateful that Stormy, the dog, had eaten the ghost and that their dear sister hadn't been shot.

Epilogue: That daughter was named Who's Who of American High School Students in the year of her graduation. She earned a degree in library science in college and now lives in Alabama with her husband and three children working for an agency of the U.S. Government.

The Two Stubborn Ones

Written February 14, 1990

In the year of 1932, Mery was born into a relatively large family of children. In her native Bolivia, she grew up as a child among Ketchua-speaking people but was educated in the Spanish language. Her father was considerably older than her mother and was a successful businessman. Both of her parents objected to her marriage when Mery fell in love with a young dentist while in her mid-twenties. That objection, however, didn't keep Mery from marrying the dentist whose name was Jorge. The parents' good judgment proved to be right, and the strong-headed girl's marriage finally dissolved.

Mery was a good mother, wife, and homemaker. During one three-year period of her marriage, she awaited her husband who was away in England studying. Anyone who knew her would attest to her fervent devotion as a Catholic. During times of worship, she would frequently put small stones in her shoes to bring pain to her feet as she made pilgrimages or walks to a favorite shrine. She made daily visits to one particular image when a son was born with a minor handicap.

The oldest of Mery's three children, a daughter named Maria, finished high school in the U.S. as an exchange student. While in her last year of high school, her daughter, Maria, came in contact with some evangelicals and was converted from her Catholic heritage. Upon returning to her native Bolivia, that daughter had little rest until she had won some of her family to her newfound faith in God. Mery, the mother, was one of those converts.

Mery's health denied her being one of those outdoor nature-loving folks. A chronic heart condition caused her to act as though she was older than her years. While she was still under 40 years old, she had open-heart surgery and not long afterward, she was baptized. Family and friends all loved the kind-hearted Mery with frail health. They were thoughtful to devote time and favors upon her whenever they could. One morning, a husband and wife couple needed Mery's knowledgeable help on a trip away from the city. That couple, Ruth and Sadnov, left the city with Mery and headed toward the Valley of Zongo where Mery's older son and family lived. She was acting as the guide on the trip of more than two hours away. Mery's friends, Ruth and Sadnov, had never been to the Zongo Valley before and had to trust her directions.

The jeep with its three passengers gently bounced over the dirt road after leaving the cobblestone streets of the city of La Paz. The elevation was gradually increasing as they headed toward the mountains. There was a mountain pass of more than 14,000 feet that had to be made before making an abrupt descent downward into the Zongo Valley. Mery seemed a little unsure of the route, but Ruth's husband knew some of those roads even though he had never been to the Zongo Valley before.

They arrived at a crossroads, and Mery said that they should turn right. "Are you sure?" asked the driver. "This road goes to Chacalataya, the ski mountain. I've been there a few times, and I don't remember a turn off anywhere from this road." With total assurance, Mery knew she was right, and the driver turned upgrade for more low-gear mountain climbing in the jeep. Hoping that Mery was right and he was wrong, Ruth's husband resigned himself to climb in the direction of what he knew to be the Mount Chacalataya route. The mountain is known to have the highest ski slope on earth. From many places over the world, skiers have gone to conquer its steep slopes and the lung-expanding, thin frigid air. Skiing there is notoriously dangerous, and accidents have claimed many injuries and lives as well.

The distance wasn't great for they were at the foot of the mountain when they turned off their route. It was the constant climbing and curve turning on the narrowest road imaginable that changed Mery's mind within a few minutes. For all practical purposes, those that go up to ski do so in the morning and then make their departure in the afternoon before a possible night snow cuts them off from the world. The road wasn't made for passing another vehicle, and truly it was almost impossible to do so.

"We better turn around for this can't be the road," said Mery. "We can't do that for the road isn't wide enough," he replied. "Have you ever been to the ski slope?" he asked. "No, I haven't, and my heart condition won't permit me to go to that altitude," she said. After a moment he asked, "How do you feel now, Mery?" "I feel all right, but I'm afraid to go to Chacalataya," she replied. Ruth's husband wasn't interested in what Mery wanted or didn't want at that point in their upward climbing. They were already within a few hundred yards by altitude of the end of the road. It just seemed to be so much farther because of the constant winding back and forth around the mountain to gain a few more feet of altitude.

"You just relax and breathe deeply until I can find a place to turn this jeep around. You'll make it all right if you stay calm," he assured her. Mery was quiet as they approached the end of the road. Suddenly the jeep passed a gate as they entered into the parking lot that marked the end of the trip.

"How do you feel now, Mery?" asked the jeep driver as he surveyed the few other vehicles that had made the trip that day. "I feel fairly well," she said. "Well," he replied, "we have room here to turn around and go back, but before we do, just open the door and put your feet on the ground." "Oh yes," he added, "from this day forward, you can brag for the rest of your life that you visited Chacalataya."

As they turned back to descend the mountain by the narrow road with its many curves, Mery was assured that she had performed courageously. "Just in case you didn't know," his voice rose above the high RPM of the jeep's motor, "you are leaving the official altitude of 17,318 feet above sea level." Mery was content as they began the downward drive after her life's one and only visit to Chacalataya.

She had lived many years within the towering view of the beautiful snow-covered Andean Mountain and had never dreamed that she could put her feet upon it. As a youth, Mery's strong-headed marriage decision brought a sad end to what every person dreams for in a marriage. On the day of Mery's trip with Ruth and Sadnov, after starting up the wrong road, it was Sadnov's strong-headed design that she do what she had always known to be impossible. She retained her designation as trip guide and finally chose the right road to the Valley of Zongo.

Stairway Marathon

Written September 27, 1989

Prologue: While it is possible that some would rather glory in physical weakness, definitely there are others that take great pride in their strength and endurance. Two men who represent two generations found themselves locked in a duel that neither intended to lose.

Jaime was no stranger to hard work and could operate any kind of road-building equipment made. He was under 40 by a few years, well above six-feet tall, and he carried the posture that a Spanish bullfighter would envy. While he and a friend were visiting a South American country, his host was putting into Jaime's schedule of limited travel time a fast pace of going. Jaime, the tall vacationer, paid all travel expenses, and his host was thoroughly enjoying the task of making Jaime's vacation a full one.

Driving across the Andean Mountains for more than seven hours one night to the city of La Paz, they were back at the host's home base. Four adults were in the small Toyota jeep. They had reservations at the airport for a 9 a.m. flight the next morning. After making a non-stop drive, they arrived between 4 a.m. and 5 a.m. in La Paz and parked in the apartment building's basement parking area. They were happy for the prospect of a few hours of rest.

That apartment building was 25 stories high, if you were to count the two levels under ground. It was at the lowest level that they parked the car. From that point, the host's wife and Jaime's friend took a suitcase each and headed for the elevator. They promptly ascended to the 22nd floor to open the apartment and heat some water for coffee. There were no restaurants for coffee stops on the mountain road they had passed over.

127

Jaime's accomplice in this South American visit had definite plans to move to Bolivia within a couple of years. He was not an absolute novice for he had already spent a few weeks in the nation with his wife on a previous visit. He knew where he was, was well acquainted with the host family, and was comfortable enough to start making his preparations for bed. He wanted to sleep the few remaining hours before leaving again.

Back down in the basement parking area, Jaime and the host were putting away the gasoline bottles that are a part of any motorist's travel gear in the Andean Mountains. After quickly locking up everything, each man grabbed a suitcase and started straight for the elevator. They couldn't have been more than two minutes behind the first two.

Tired arms rested the suitcases on the floor while awaiting the elevator. It was returning from its last stop on the 22nd floor. No one else would have been using it at that hour in the night. Time ran out to exceed the necessary minute or two for it to come. When punching the call button again, they observed that it didn't light up. Obviously it wasn't working. There were four elevators in the building located at different points, so they went to another and were confronted with the same response. Locking their suitcases back in the car, the two ascended a flight of stairs to check the elevator at another level. They were tired and sleepy men and weren't interested in any Halloween pranks. The elevator was functioning minutes before because they saw the first two get on. If that were a prank then the two basement dwellers were ready for the pranksters to get their jollies full and restore power to the elevators.

Time was passing, and they both wanted and needed some rest. In scarcely more than four hours, they were going to be flying out, and it was not the appropriate time for practical jokes. Soon they became aware that they were going from one side of the building to the other just wasting the precious little strength and time they had left. If the elevators had genuinely failed, which had been known to happen, then they needed to be heading up the dark stairway toward the 22nd floor.

Now Jaime's host and wife had lived in La Paz, the world's highest capital city, for 12 years. The couple could scarcely remember how long they had already been gray. There was, however, still an advantage or two left to them. Their lungs were as accustomed as they would ever be to the thin air of the 13,000 feet above sea level where they lived. There was the red corpuscle build up in the blood, which is normal for altitude dwellers. Jaime's host wasn't frightened by the prospect of having to walk up to the 22nd floor, which were fully 24 flights of stairs from the basement. He did look more favorably toward other means of recreation, however. Besides all that, he felt that he had already had his recreation for the day.

Jaime neither displayed anguish or fear. The suggestion of the high walk in the night didn't seem to trouble him at all. They were still empty-handed since locking up their suitcases in the car. Taking the lead up the dark stairs was the white-headed man, but Jaime was never more than two treads behind.

Up in the apartment by this time, Jaime's travel buddy was in his pajamas and house robe. He and the host's wife, a much older woman, had made numerous openings of the apartment door just to check on the other two. They should have already arrived from below. Indeed they listened for sounds and even had begun to call as loudly as they dared in the building. While they stood outside the apartment door for the two stragglers, Jaime's friend went half way up the last remaining flight of stairs toward an unfinished apartment above. He called out, "Come on out, Jaime, we know you're up there." There was no sign or sound of the last two weary travelers. One coded for the elevator knowing by that time something had happened.

When it didn't respond, they then realized that the delay was no joke. If one question had been answered, there were others whose answers were yet to come.

While the two fortunate elevator riders stood silent vigil, high on the 22nd floor, the stragglers were breathing hard with hearts pumping double time coming up the stairway. If they had started out taking two treads at a time, it was already cut back to one by the time the sentries high above heard those first faint gaspings for air.

The stairway soldiers were making a forced march in complete silence, except for their laboring lungs. Red eyes for want of sleep, dry mouth and throat, and parched lips were not deemed as sufficient reason for a pause to either. It was hurtful, though, that their lungs burned for oxygen. Neither of the stairway climbers had asked the other to stop or pause for a breath, but for sure both had wanted to. The floor numbers got larger and their breathing got louder, and no one was saying a word. For age difference, they could have been father and son, but the two were men in their own right and neither intended for a stairway to deny him from being the best.

The wife above in hushed words said to Jaime's friend that she wasn't going to be available to either ask or explain anything when her husband arrived. He was going to be absolutely furious. Jaime's friend took the suggestion as good counsel from a superior and quickly retired to his sleeping quarters.

The two men were too breathless and too weary to do more than grunt a good night. Each fully understood the plight of the other as they retired to their bedrooms for a little rest. A minute or two passed as the host to the vacationers was preparing for bed, and all was silent as his wife feigned to be asleep. With enough pretense to make it all seem real, she startled awake to give ear to a thoroughly disgusted husband's bedtime remark. "I wasn't going to let that "red neck" from Mississippi walk me down coming up the stairs."

In the other bedroom at the same moment, Jaime triumphantly was bidding good night to his friend with a similar remark. "There's no way that I was going to let that old white-headed man walk off and leave me sitting on that stairway."

~~~~~~~~~~~~~~~~~~~~~~~~~~~

Gregoria's Sweet 26

Written November 10, 1989

A family of four arrived in South America after receiving a church assignment as missionaries. Their ability to speak Spanish rated from poor to worse, and this considerably restricted any maneuvering around in their new place of residence. The ground floor apartment they chose to rent was close to their language institute, but that wasn't all. It was accessible to lots of beggars, sales people, and domestic job seekers as well. So many of these folks were always ringing the door bell that they decided to hire a maid to help answer the door and say "no."

There was no shortage of applicants from which to choose. Most had some kind of letter, falsified or real, to recommend them as hard working, honest, and dependable. The family of foreigners in their Spanish surroundings tried to choose wisely, so a young woman was chosen who had a letter, dressed neatly, and was bilingual. The householders conducted an interview to gain more information, and even with the best that they could do, the chosen young woman remained a complete stranger.

Though a person may speak five languages, only one is his and the other four are borrowed. The young woman's name was Gregoria and spoke Aymara as her native language, but she also spoke Spanish. Both the employed maid and the householders had to communicate in their second languages, and understandably there were innocent errors and difficulties. She was 26 years old, a ready talker, had enough extra weight to be called stout, possessed a good sense of humor, and was a good cook.

The new residents had much to learn besides a new language and all didn't come easy or without shock. One troubling thing was that rental contracts were private documents and didn't really mean a lot. This is to say that the landlord could toss them out almost indiscriminately in the high-inflation climate of that time. People buying and selling rental houses circumvented government rental regulations, and each transaction was accompanied with an increase in rent to the occupants. Those who didn't know the ploy of those landlords found themselves moving quite frequently. What the landlord truly wanted was an increase in rent to keep up with the inflation, so the new residents that didn't know these tricks had to keep moving. The rental house buying and selling was a landlord's hoax.

Where did Gregoria figure into this whole scheme? In two successive moves over a period of a few months, the family that employed Gregoria was depending on her for some of her able strength. That stout young woman, amiable with a charming personality, good cook, and pleasant talker would always get sick and be bedfast during the family's move to new quarters. As a result, Gregoria began to lose some of her worth as a dependable employee.

In the course of time, another family arrived from the U.S. that needed a helper in their home. This was a good opportunity for the first family to find a nice position for dear Gregoria. She had served her time well for their family with the broom, pots and pans, and answering the door. It was furlough time for Gregoria's first employer, and everything worked out well as she was switched to another home.

With the return after a year in the U.S. of Gregoria's first employer, they learned that the dear maid was living in another city. Not long afterward, the second family chose to leave the country, and this left the maid without employment. Without a job, dear Gregoria, the maid, began to search for the first employer family, and she found them to her true delight. It was a surprise to the first family for by that time it had been nearly six years since she was given the original job to answer the apartment door and say "no" to sales people, job seekers, some beggars, and a variety of solicitors. Language barriers had been solved, and the North Americans had rejected the status symbol of having to keep a maid to be considered first class. Besides, there were no longer any children at home.

When she found the first employer family, they began to reminiscence their years together. They talked of the typical dishes Gregoria had introduced into the home, new and different shopping places, excursions into the country, and various new experiences that were mutual to them. It was all so memorable and pleasant to recall the times and places together, and they talked on about the good days when they were together.

When conversation began to lose some of its rapid pace, and they began to think for something to talk about, the man of the house asked a question. "Gregoria, how old are you now?" With her ready smile that accentuated her white teeth in the setting of her dark brown face, she replied, "I'm around 26 years old."

~~~~~~~~~~~~~~~~~~~~~~~~~~~~~~~~~~~~~

Brave Dad with Crying Dog

Written September 25, 1989

<u>*Prologue:*</u> *Valor and bravery seem to be emotions that display themselves at unpredictable times and in uncertain ways. When an emergency calls for action, a person may become a hero or perhaps become a coward.*

Sadnov's wife was away to attend the bedside of her desperately ill mother. He was the home keeper alone, and this was an uncommon thing during their 40 years of marriage. Sadnov wasn't plagued with paranoia, but there were things he enjoyed more than having to stay alone in the house at night. Dita was the house dog, and she was a good informer when someone rang the doorbell. No one could call her a real house protector, though, just because she had ears for doorbells. Out in the yard that was walled in was a big dog named Oso. Oso is the Spanish word for bear. The only thing lacking in Oso was that he didn't have any of the furious nature of a bear. He was only a big barking dog, and alas, he had taken up the most undesirable habit of wailing in the night. His crying wail had already brought remarks from two different neighbors who grew tired of hearing him in the night.

This was the general situation that necessitated phone calls and letters from one lonely Sadnov in order to stay in touch with his family a few thousand miles away. In a letter to one of their daughters during those days of his loneliness, he mentioned their dog Oso and his night howling. Here you have a quotation from that letter that proves that heroism can be born out of the wind.

Vondas A. Smith

"I need to get back on the Sunday lesson preparation for tomorrow and try to get up the nerve to sleep by myself tonight. Two nights ago, I had the second-story bedroom window open to call the crying dog down every few minutes out in the yard. I dropped back asleep with the window open, and the wind came through and slammed the bedroom door like a bomb. I came out of the bed with enough adrenaline in my blood to kill a herd of bull elephants barehanded. I found myself out in the hallway wanting someone to fight. I think I made enough noise inside to scare the dog on the outside."

~~~~~~~~~~~~~~~~~~~~~~~~~~~~

Colón Street Beggar

Written November 16, 1989

Begging is a necessity for some, and to some, it is a profession. There are those that have developed it into a fine art in many parts of the developing world where it is the only means of survival for a visible portion of the population. Beggars are often very old and handicapped; however, some are scarcely past walking age with the mother sitting inconspicuously close by. There is always the artist or "con man," and it would be futile to try to fit him into a particular type. He is so versatile and elusive that his tactics, more often than not, are not obvious to a would-be giver.

No society has escaped absolutely from having some of these unfortunate souls, and it is unfortunate for society. In at least one capital city in Latin America, motorists stopping at traffic signals have to keep their car windows raised. Tourists leaving their hotels almost need to be wearing running shoes. The post office, market places, and money exchange houses are to be named among a number of places where beggars periodically work. Some pretend to sell something while others make no pretense at anything. They are even known to become angry at times if the coin or gift is too insignificant.

There was one beggar who never lost his self-respect. He was a permanent fixture on the south side of Colón Street in a major city of Bolivia. In his one block area, where other beggars did not dare to intrude, he was the monarch. The Sudamer Money Exchange House was scarcely more than 100 feet from where he would be propped against a building and leaning forward on his crutches. He was smooth shaven each morning before he went to town to take up his post. His clothing was faded but always clean. He never wore rags and did not have in hand a pan or hat in which to receive contributions. He wore a hat that was befitting his attire.

The beggar of Colón Street did not fit the beggar's image, but he was a beggar. He did not step away from his restful "propped-up leaning" position to ask alms of everyone. He was selective. As customers entered the money exchange house close by, the sharp eye of the crippled man was always observing. He would make sure that any obviously foreign-dressed people would have an opportunity to assist him with a gift. The town's people knew him, and he knew them as well.

Marcus was a young son of a new family in town and obviously a foreigner to the people on the street. Like some American parents, they gave Marcus an allowance of spending money, not much but some. As Marcus accompanied his mother in town one day, they passed the crippled man's place on Colón Street. Out stepped the crippled man. His face bore the grimace of a tortured one, and on his crutches, he moved like a man painfully handicapped. Marcus' heart was smitten as he viewed such a sad and hapless man. In an instant he knew, that with his relatively plenty, he could become the benefactor of a poor wretched soul. Without a need to think, young Marcus handed over a week's allowance and walked away delighted that he made the crippled man's day a bit brighter.

With the passing of time, the man on crutches began to be viewed with a suspicious eye by Marcus. Now that Marcus was a resident and ventured into the streets more often, he wondered why the beggar was so selective with the folks from which he begged. In the home Marcus would refer to the man on crutches as "Deep Throat." This nickname came from the teen-ager because of the beggar's exceptionally low tone of voice.

One day, after checking the post office and making a small purchase in town, Marcus arrived home at the closing of the business day. He was so angry he could not contain his emotions. "Say, don't ever give another cent to "Ole Deep Throat" down on Colón Street," he told his mother. "Why?" she asked. "Because "Ole Deep Throat" is a fake," Marcus said. "Why would you call that dear old man a fake, son?" implored his mother. "Because I just saw him leaving downtown a little while ago, walking down the street with his crutches under his arm!"

~~~~~~~~~~~~~~~~~~~~~~~~~~~~~~~

Vondas A. Smith

Too Impatient for Prudence

Written September 16, 1989

Prologue: There are a few things that happen only once in a lifetime, and some of those shouldn't be told. Here is one that brought voluntary silence between the man of the house and the family maid.

The mid-September day was warm, and the southern hemisphere spring was just a few days away. It was Monday, and a missionary couple in a foreign country had just had an exceptionally busy weekend. Time was devoted on the previous Saturday night to conducting a wedding. Sunday's activities are always the most important of the week, and added to their usual busy day, the previous Sunday was an afternoon given to planning another wedding. After church on the same Sunday night, a sick call in a home became much more than a routine call. A nurse had to be obtained for the night and pain shots administered every four hours. The patient's illness was terminal, and the end was nearer than they had thought, so the tired missionary couple devoted much of the night to help.

Without much explanation, it is understandable why the missionary thought that Monday would be a rest day. Nearly all day he did exactly what he wanted to do. He started by fixing his own breakfast, put the dog out, and tended to a pet parrot. He then dug around some rose bushes, talked to a neighbor, and watered the lawn. He examined new burrows in the yard where mice were staking out new claims. The plum tree, which had begun to show its tiny green fruit, was given his special attention with the water hose.

Their uneventful day about home on that Monday was lovely until a call came from a neighboring pastor's wife across town. The caller asked the missionary wife if permission would be granted for them to invite themselves over to the missionary's home for an evening of fellowship and to spend the night with them. The missionary wife, an older woman, did not know how to say "no" or wait until another time. It was sure that the unsolicited visitors would not fail to show up. Another call then came during mid-afternoon from the family of the desperately ill woman. The second call sent the missionary wife with the maid out on a search for medicine and food to serve the coming visitors. A student nurse was found that would be in attendance at the bedside of the sick woman for the night. The husband continued to jealously feel that he was entitled to his day; however, he did politely listen to his wife's suggestion that he curtail his activities with plenty of time remaining to get ready to receive the coming guests.

"I should be home by 6 p.m.," she said with her parting instructions. Part of those instructions was that he should finish his chores and clean up by that time. He was in full agreement and began watching his time. Neither of them would have thought that she would have encountered any delay in completing her chores in the time that she allotted herself.

Very dutifully, the time-watching husband was just finishing his shower at 5:30 p.m. The telephone hand set was within reach so that no phone call would be missed. Everything was carefully attended to. The right door was locked so that the wife could enter with her house key should he still be in the shower when she arrived. His house robe, shoes, and towel were laid out in order, and he was about to turn off the shower when it happened.

There was a powerful unapologetic knocking at the door. "Why would she knock at the door?" he thought. He knew she had the key. Without making any special haste, the shower was turned off, and he reached for the bath towel. He knew she would use her house key even if it brought a complaint from her later. He was wishing she would go on and do it without waiting for him. The knocking came again and seemed to be even more urgent and louder than the first time. He was almost stubbornly slow and made no effort to rush to her call to open the door. She then returned to the yard gate to use the house buzzer button and give a nice long ring. Enough was enough. She had arrived early, disturbed his peaceful shower, and now wasn't civil enough to show the least bit of patience.

He performed a hurried swipe of the bath towel across his dripping wet head. He then took the towel directly to his feet only to keep from getting his house shoes wet and making wet footprints on the waxed floor. Anything more than that would be left to the slow process of air-drying.

In one flinging move, the large blue bath towel became a wrap around his hips and mid body. Off to the door, he marched taking only a few seconds to cross two rooms to the wife's urgent summons. He was set to do two things: the first was to open the door to his wife, and the second was to start denouncing her before she could open her mouth. He succeeded in doing the first.

There was no delay in getting the door open for the key was readily available. There was a harsh greeting on his lips as he snatched it open, but a ton of silence tied his tongue. He was nearly blinded with embarrassment and a camera-like imprint was stamped on his brain.

The unforgettable photo that burned into his picture-tube brain was that of the housemaid standing silently with a mound of full shopping bags from the grocery market. The wife had dropped her off at the house and hastened off for another urgent errand for the sick woman.

Neither spoke a word, but the door that was snatched open was swiftly closed. He tightened his hold on the big blue towel about himself and turned away to forget his harsh greeting. He was hoping that the maid in the red blouse standing at the door would forget some things also.

The Burial Secret

Written November 27, 1989

Prologue: Two men from vastly different cultures were communicating by using their second languages. One was a native English speaker, and the other's native language was Aymara. Since they both spoke Spanish, it was in this language that they always communicated together.

Sadnov had been in the United States for a full year on furlough, and during the time that he was away, his Spanish began to need some practice. Upon his return to work again in Bolivia, though needing some of that practice, he was immediately thrust into full-time activities again.

The phone rang late one afternoon, and the caller was Sadnov's long-time friend. The voice was distraught denoting that there was deep grief in the heart of the caller. Gregorio, the long-time friend, made that call and through tears related the death of his brother, Pascual. Sadnov was deeply touched by the grief of a friend whose brother had suddenly died. Indeed Sadnov promised to hurriedly get ready and go to the home where the body would be kept that night. Sadnov made his appearance and found that many relatives had already gathered at the wake.

With quiet mannerisms, Sadnov greeted those of the bereaved family who had arrived. Some family members, not well known to him, had already come to the city from the country. He looked for the widow of the deceased but was unable to recognize her in the presence of the large family. Anyway, it was for Gregorio that he had made his hurried visit. Gregorio had lost a brother and, indeed, he and his brother were close. They lived in the same house with their families and both of them worked for the same company.

Gregorio's brother, in life, was active in his church and was always up front as the song director. He was a quiet man and had many friends.

During a short memorial service that night in the home, scripture selections were read which were accompanied with some brief remarks. All was purposefully done, including prayers, for the surviving widow and the other members of the deceased's immediate family. Gregorio's name was called in prayer before the Lord for strength and comfort during his time of great grief. He had lost a younger brother who was very precious to him.

Since there is almost no embalming of the dead, and certainly no laws to that practice, it is necessary to bury the dead within 48 hours. The next day, as the coffin was hoisted on the shoulders of the pallbearers, others took up the flowers into their arms, and the considerably large company of mourners marched away to the cemetery. It was a fairly common sight, but it never ceases to be an impressive one. Down the road they marched quietly, with women veiled in black, depicting that they were in mourning. This custom is ancient among Latinos. Often times it isn't easy to distinguish the women apart for they are all dressed alike in their black mourning attire.

Sadnov, as a near friend to Gregorio, marched at his side as they moved on to the burial. He commented that he had never lost a brother, and assured Gregorio that he did care and certainly offered prayers for his comfort and strength during this time.

The burial was in a vault at a mausoleum. It wasn't a new one, and the bones of the former burial had already been removed before they arrived. When the large company of mourners arrived with Sadnov at Gregorio's side, they did not pass by the chapel for the Catholic burial rites. They went directly to their assigned burial place.

Some of those in attendance were from another congregation, and at least two were women. They had been informed that Gregorio's brother was to be buried, and they wanted to attend. There they were, one named Pocha and another named Maria. When the opportunity presented itself, both women assured Sadnov that the man that led songs in church was alive and well and in their midst. "No," said Sadnov. "He is dead and in that coffin." It was Pocha who said, "But over there is the one that is the song leader in their church." Sadnov assured her that it did look like him but in the family there were other brothers and some of them looked alike. The two women were not convincing Sadnov.

The coffin was lifted to the small opening and pushed to the full depth of the vault. An employee of the cemetery began to mix some plaster as another carefully placed some brick in order. With the soft plaster, covering the brick, the tomb was sealed. Sadnov was viewing from a short distance, but looking on from a side view, he could not see everything clearly. Using a small pencil like instrument in the soft plaster, a cemetery employee wrote the name of the deceased. In addition, he wrote the date of birth and death. The last words were written, as Sadnov looked on, "She was the wife of Pascual Peña."

To this day it isn't known if Gregorio needs to learn English or if perhaps Sadnov should learn Aymara. Sadnov had conducted the funeral for one person while the burial was for another.

~~~~~~~~~~~~~~~~~~~~~~~~~~~~~~~

Vondas A. Smith

Mountain Folks Go To Town

Written December 7, 1989

Prologue: No one would think it unreasonable to say that an expecting mother is as big and heavy on the day before giving birth as she'll ever be. Suppose that she feigned to have labor pains on that day. Who is the person from a crowd of many faces that would be able to distinguish the fact from fiction?

A man and wife traveling together on a dirt road in the mountains of Bolivia had just finished a particularly difficult part of their trip. They were relieved to have their jeep back on the paved asphalt section of the road. There were still 2 ½ hours left for them to drive on the route that never has a scarcity of hitchhikers. At the end of the dirt-road section, a mandatory stop was made for a police check of their authorization papers to travel. As the husband finished the momentary routine with the police check and was about to drive off, a man ran up to him in real anguish. His fright and worry didn't need a lengthy explanation. Following him was a woman, said to be his wife, who had already began to have her first labor pains in birth. There was no doctor in that remote section of the mountains.

Though the traveling jeep driver and wife were in agreement to never carry unknown people, this was a troubling situation. Saying "no" was common to young and old folks alike. The negative response was as easy to women and children as it was to men and boys. The risk was simply too great. Once he had refused to pick up two military men who had just wrecked their jeep. Indeed the traveling couple was troubled over what they should do.

The driver of the jeep looked at the grimace on the pregnant woman's face—obviously in pain—and consented to help. Picking up hitchhikers—the very thing that he and his wife had always agreed not to do—now became acceptable. They picked up two complete strangers and hoped that they would still be two when they finished their trip. The speed limit was only dictated by weather, road, and vehicle conditions. All three categories were ideal for a fast trip, and off they went to the hospital. "I hope this little newcomer can wait until I get them to the hospital," the man said to his wife. "What do we do if she starts giving birth?" asked his wife. "You'll have to answer that, because I don't know," he responded. "I've done lots of things but never have I, nor do I want to, fill in as a pediatrician or mid-wife." With that remark he added another five kilometers per hour to his fast pace of driving.

The pregnant woman's man, or husband, was as calm as a cucumber but the woman was restless. The two of them were instructed to sit on the floor in the back of the little jeep. In that position they were in no risk of being thrown from the seat on the tight curves. Tires were squealing in the curves of the asphalt roadway. The center of gravity on the relatively high-top jeep isn't low enough to be ideal for working curves at high speed. The traffic was somewhat light, and the driver began to cheat on the curves as much as he dared. About the only thing more that could be done was to throw their weight into the curves with a change of sitting position. That may or may not have helped a little.

"How is she acting now?" he asked his wife in English. "She just had a hard pain," she answered. "How close do they seem to be?" he asked again. "I'm only using the rearview mirror, and it may be that I'm not catching her face expressions every time," she said. "I sure hope we can make that hospital," said the husband. He was holding the pedal to the medal to gain velocity for the next hill.

They had no shortage of gasoline, but he was just a little apprehensive about the brakes. Mountain driving and hot brakes need to be kept as far apart as possible. Those mountains were well populated with small memorial crosses in the curves that indicate fatalities that occurred on that spot. Their fast mission in the jeep was hoped to bring a life into the world, not usher one or some out of it. Staying off the brakes as much as possible, he kept a high motor RPM whether going up or down.

"According to her face, she is in a hard labor pain right now," said the wife. "Check the time and watch her close for the next pain," he said. Again he added, "Honestly, I can't do any better than what I'm doing in getting us there." "Don't try any harder," said the wife, "you've got me so scared, I forget to watch the woman."

The last descent from the mountains was a long one, and never had it been more welcomed than it was during that hot afternoon by one jeep driver and his wife. After reaching the valley, their travel distance was still just over 40 kilometers to the city and the much-needed hospital. Racing along the flat valley roadway was a help to take the edge off their throbbing nerves. The right rear tire was found to be just a little short of air, but a fast check didn't find it too hot to not be able to go farther.

The English-speaking travelers darted across town to the Hospital Vedma. A doctor friend of theirs, Dr. Juan Mendoza, did a lot of practice at that hospital. His emergency flashers on the jeep were working, and the traffic law was set aside for the simplest set of safety rules. Reaching the main gate of the hospital without the expectant mother having given birth was a gift of mercy from God.

The driver desperately wanted the man and the expectant mother out, and he conveniently parked at the main door of the hospital. Too relieved for words, he leaped out and had the back door open nearly before the hitchhiking couple knew where they were. Slowly they stirred from the floor of the jeep and got out. Reaching back for a medium-sized bundle of belongings brought the end to the dangerous mission of mercy.

Beside the jeep stood the driver needing a treatment for nerve exhaustion and a cool place to park the jeep to let the tires cool down. The scene that took place before him was unspeakable. Incredulously, he watched the cucumber-cool man and the huge mother-in-waiting—with the face that unmistakably displayed unbearable pain—walk calmly away. With unbelieving solitude, the driver and his wife watched the two hitchhikers walk under the huge arch of the drive-in gate to the hospital. Once on the outside of the hospital grounds, they were immediately lost in the pedestrian-populated street.

Without doubt, a Bolivian-mountain couple laughs today when they think of their taxi ride to town in the style of "most-favored customer." While that couple laughs, there is a particular driver and his wife that have once again entered into their vows not to pick up strangers. For the next act of labor pains, he hopes to have on hand a box of aspirin.

Vondas A. Smith

Carney's Short Cut

Written November 17, 1989

Early one afternoon in a small Toyota sedan, four adults were speeding along on a mountain road in the South American Andes. They were from a southern state in the U.S. and had lots in common. Two were newly arrived visitors to that Andean nation of Bolivia while the other two were long-time residents. The visitors were busy with cameras, chasing views of the llamas and alpacas. There were no gaps in conversation even after being on the road for four hours. Perhaps another three hours remained of their trip, but they were enjoying every moment of time together.

Meeting or passing another vehicle on the road meant that windows were raised to avoid the high density of dust coming into the car. There were sufficient begging children along the roadway, and after the elevation reached above 13,000 feet, there was little or nothing growing out of the dust and rocks of the mountains. There were oohs and aahs, and a lively conversation all the way.

One of the men was named Carney, which means "meat" in Spanish. He had told the driver named Sadnov that he would make a good dirt-track race driver. Sadnov was performing quite well, but there was a good reason. He had driven that road for some years and knew it well. He knew the unwritten codes of mountain driving and how to and where to look for danger. He pointed out places of some bad accidents of trucks and buses and told of seeing blanket-covered bodies of those victims lying at accident scenes on the side of the road.

The South American summer rains bring mountain slides occasionally, which can slightly alter the road route. On that long section of road, which had no paving or improvement of any kind, the drivers themselves sometimes work out alternate routes to cut off a few winding curves. One of these shortcuts, as it may be called, had a steep drop from the road level going in the direction that they were traveling.

Sadnov was losing no time and kept his speed to the maximum that would still be considered by him as safe. The party-style conversation was as lively as ever. Suddenly, Sadnov came upon a favorite shortcut. Without a thought of the two in the rear seat or a word of announcement, he pulled the car sharply to the left off the level roadway. The vehicle nosed down into an exceptionally sharp drop and into an unusually heavy carpet of loose dirt. Immediately, a blinding cloud of dust rose to engulf the vehicle, giving them a feeling of disorientation and a sense of falling over the mountainside from the roadway.

The deep roadway dust, obscuring the frontal vision, caused Sadnov to reduce speed quickly. It was too late for Carney to sit up to observe. He had already dropped to the floor and positioned himself for a long fall, which subconsciously to him meant death. He had left the seat impulsively in a fractional second and wedged his long physical frame in the floor of the small Toyota sedan. He was so tightly folded that he could scarcely breathe and was too scared to want to breathe anyway. When he realized within a second or two that they were still on a roadway, he began to cry out, "My heart, my heart!"

Amid the laughter of the others, Carney's back seat companion, a stout man named Tim, began to help him get his long legs and body unfolded from his position in the floor. Tim artfully got him to swallow his heart back into place again.

The incident will never be forgotten by any of the four. It has been told and retold by each of them a number of times. Today, Carney's Bolivian friends call that section of the Andean Mountain road as "Carney's Cut."

Vondas A. Smith

His survival of the episode made him an older man, and he probably wishes that Sadnov were too.

~~~~~~~~~~~~~~~~~~~~~~~~~~~~~~~~~~~~~

Girl Scout Finds a Way

Written July 22, 1998

Maria was the first born of three children in her family, and while she was a young student in an all-girl parochial school, she became a Girl Scout. She, the little Bolivian Girl Scout, was young and very small during one especially bloody military overthrow of the government in her country. As a Scout, she was once assigned the horrendous task of fitting bodies of fallen countrymen brought in off the streets during that bloody uprising into odd-shaped wooden coffins and boxes. The boxes for burial were scarce, and there were many bodies, so she and others had to find a way to fit as many into a burial box as possible.

When Maria became a teenager, she began to find new comfort and hope in life through the message of an evangelical movement that grew widespread in her country in the early part of the 1970s. She spent three days in jail once when police mistakenly thought their evangelical meetings were political rallies. When about to finish high school, Maria received a scholarship to become a foreign exchange student and finish high school in the United States. This she did in Houston, Texas. In addition to her diploma from high school in Houston, she was finally baptized there which caused her former religious heritage to become history.

Upon returning to her native country from the United States in 1975, Maria faced formidable opposition in her family for her newfound religion. She was a little older, wiser, and very zealous for her newfound faith in God. Anxious to lead her family to experience her Christian joy, she rejoined the family in her home in La Paz, Bolivia.

One day, while she and her family sat around the table eating and chatting, Maria learned from her dentist father that he had performed some

153

dental work for the daughter of a missionary from the United States. This was most interesting to Maria. She had been told by some of her acquaintances in Houston about a newly arrived North American missionary family in her country. She was told the family's name and was advised by her Houston church friends to find them when she returned to her country.

At an appropriate time with the family together, Maria asked, "Dad, what is the name of the girl patient that can't speak Spanish, and where does she live?" "I can't remember," said her father. "What does she look like?" asked Maria. He began to draw a verbal picture of the foreign girl according to his best memory. "Dad, do you want me to tell you her family name?" asked Maria. "You don't know her," he responded. "No, I do not, but her name is Smith, and I shall know her," said Maria. She left her dad completely speechless for he recognized the name upon hearing it again.

To protect the privacy of his patient, the dentist father would not let Maria into his office files to find an address or phone number for the missionary family. This was meant to be his ethical way to protect his client's privacy. His only accomplishment in this was to achieve a delay of a few days. Maria knew what she wanted, and she waited with patience for an opportunity to go through the files when her father was out of the office. Maria was bilingual, and the missionary daughter was not, so Maria felt a compulsion to find her.

The city of La Paz was inhabited by a million people and is large in area. With a phone number and address, Maria called and learned that the Smiths lived amazingly close. Having received an invitation from the new family, Maria took a short taxi ride and within a half-hour they were together.

Each one rejoiced to be a party to a miracle on that day in May 1975, in the living room of an apartment located in Plaza Isabel La Católica, in the city of La Paz. The little things, jubilantly insignificant, the first thoughts, and suggestions were unknowingly made that gradually multiplied and have grown to become a church that is vibrant in every state, except one, of the republic of Bolivia. Maria located the newly arrived family who ultimately dedicated nearly 23 years of missionary labors in her country, baptizing numbers of her family, and ordaining one of her brothers to the ministry. Maria, the Girl Scout, found a way!

Wilderness Hero, City Despicable

Written July 4, 1998

Howard and his wife had already spent a day on the road—at least seven hours—and fully half of the time was spent crossing a range of the Andes. For another large portion of the day, he and his wife were flying along in his late model jeep on an easy stretch of the Altiplano, a high plain dividing two ranges of the Andean Mountains of Bolivia. His wife had gone along on that part of the trip solely for the purpose of caring for her mother who had received multiple leg fractures two months before and could not be left at home alone. Howard and his father-in-law, Ardell, would be away for an extended trip of five days into the eastern jungles to complete another phase of opening a mission church.

The second day of Howard's trip was a Wednesday, a busy one in the city of Cochabamba shopping for essentials. Some was for the trip but other things, including a 12-foot refrigerator, were to be used in a small business venture to aid the national pastor and two co-workers to support themselves as they did mission work. At the end of the second day, the jeep was heavily loaded and serviced for an early start on the following morning. It would be a long day, driving over treacherous mountains, valleys, and tropical areas. As foreigners in Bolivia, they did not savor the idea of having to pass through the nation's cocaine-producing area. Detention in those parts is more common than death, but all deaths aren't attributable to accident. Howard was relatively a newcomer to the nation's roadways, but Ardell had already survived over 22 years of that way of life, and he knew the arts of survival.

Howard and Ardell drove off from Cochabamba on the third day for him, on a long drive to Santa Cruz. Ardell was the new member on that trip, an older man, but a vital one, and Howard knew it well. They had snacks, soft drinks, and some good cassettes. There was no radio transmission strong enough to make the car radio workable. Traffic was light that day, and most of the vehicles on the road were buses, large trucks loaded with fruit and vegetables, or tractor-trailer rigs of chemical barrels going to and from the cocaine laboratories. An occasional stop had to be made at police check points to display their ID, authorization permit, and tax receipt to be on the roadway.

The day was uneventful. It was also unfruitful for them after arrival in Santa Cruz in late afternoon. They needed and wanted to get yellow fever shots before going into the jungle the next day. They didn't get the shots, but they did learn that those should have been taken two weeks before to be any benefit on their trip.

The next morning they checked out of their hotel in Santa Cruz early, bought a tank of gas, some snacks, and drove northeast for a longer day on the road to Trinidad. Neither had given any thought to the fact that it was January 31, the end of the second month of the rain season. Their calculation, though wrong, would have made it a trip of 13 hours. Even for Ardell, they were going into a new department of the nation. Neither he nor Howard had asked anyone about road conditions since the rains began, and it was so common to the local folks that it wasn't a matter of conversation. The two travelers didn't even know that it was the third consecutive day that buses had discontinued service over that route due to roadway conditions. Having known it wouldn't have changed anything except make them more apprehensive. They had gone too far to stop or turn back. It was a hot day, very humid, and the auto's air-conditioner felt good.

Less than 100 kilometers out of Santa Cruz, the asphalt highway ran out. Soon afterward they came upon a very long, single-lane bridge. The one lane for road vehicles also included railway tracks for trains. The bridge was so long and narrow they were not sure that they were seeing, or could see, the end. They looked for a traffic signal to direct traffic, and there was none. No one was on duty as a traffic controller. It was clearly left to the traveler's cunning and boldness to get on the bridge and be able to get off at the other end. They scored well on that obstacle simply because they were one of the few on the road that day. Driving off the wooden-floored bridge of loose, noisy planks seemed to inject them into another atmosphere. There came to them a strange feeling that survival was only to the fittest. The forest seemed to close in just a little closer, police outposts were farther apart, and there was less of everything that was associated with mankind. A man was seen once carrying a rifle and a big rat-like animal he had killed. Seeing the man caused the two travelers to feel so kindly toward him that they stopped just to greet him. A few words of small talk with him brought smiles, even laughter, as they drove on chatting about his accent and speech difference.

The dirt road progressively became worse with mud holes and deep ruts made by heavy vehicles. Occasionally, there was a stalled vehicle stuck in the road. Each of those was left in the care of a guard that had set up a small camping tent for his home on the road while guarding a stalled vehicle. There were short showers of rain, and then short appearances of full sun. Even when the road was higher with no holes of water or deep ruts, it was treacherously slick. They were already encountering some of those auto wheel slipups that were threatening enough to give younger drivers a road thrill. These two travelers were more interested in arriving at their destination than the thrills of roadway slipping and sliding. Their speed began to be sacrificed to the greater hazards before them, and it was evident that they were falling behind in their time schedule to be in Trinidad by 5 p.m.

It happened—not because it was inevitable—but it happened anyway. To Ardell, it had seemed inevitable. Howard did not have the double traction on his jeep engaged. He was driving a little fast, and then he jammed the full brake in a road-induced slide of the jeep. Skidding off of the roadway, they slammed into the heavy growth that skirted the road. That event had not been prepared for; however, it was not the most unfortunate either. The little that could be seen from the jeep windows was jungle growth, dripping water, and swarms of mosquitoes. Ardell had offered a few times to help as a relief driver, but Howard was enjoying himself in his new experience and declined any help. In an effort to free the jeep from the jungle's parking place, Howard engaged the four-wheel drive. Ardell, after examining the broken windshield before his face and small slivers of glass on his clothes, got out to lift a not so heavy tree branch that came to rest on the hood of the jeep. The jeep was not entrenched, nor was the tree limbs holding it back, so Howard backed out of their jungle prison relatively easy. Back on the roadway, they took cameras out to record the place and the jeep's damage. The time was 2:15 p.m. Ardell lost a drop of blood from a finger, caused by a sliver of the windshield glass, and they lost some 20 minutes driving time. Otherwise, the auto body shop could repair the rest of the damage.

It didn't seem that the road could become worse, but it did. In the lower places, the dual-wheel heavy trucks and buses left deeper ruts and holes in the muddy water that covered the road. Most of the ruts were under standing water, and it made the increasing danger to their heavily loaded small vehicle invisible. As they drove over the road that seemed to be as wide as a football field, it was anybody's guess which side of the road was the safest one to drive on. Howard guessed wrong at a particular place about two hours after landing them in the jungle. The jeep jolted to a dead stop while they drove through some deep water. Despair fell upon them, and questions without answers flooded their minds. Neither was qualified to speak rationally of their dilemma. He unsuccessfully tried to move it forward and then rearward only to cease his efforts after a few minutes. There they sat quietly with the motor still running. That was when Ardell told him to turn the engine off and save gas. There was a long pause without a word as they contemplated their situation. Rafael Lima was expecting them in Trinidad by 5 p.m., and they were already hours behind schedule and completely stalled.

Howard broke the silence as he looked at Ardell and asked, "Do you want to try it?" Ardell had already offered his service a number of times, and he was quietly vexed over Howard's lack of driving skills in the backcountry. His driving expertise, learned as a youth on the streets of Detroit, should have been left back in Detroit when he took up residence in Bolivia. He hadn't done that, and now in trouble a second time in the same afternoon, he wanted someone to bail him out. Nevertheless, being totally bogged down in the road, hours from their destination, someone had to help. Ardell quietly replied without anxiousness, "Yeah, I'll try."

Riding with Howard for two days already, Ardell got his first chance to drive. The jeep was completely stalled deep in the wilderness. What a privilege! At the time, Ardell felt more like leaving Howard with his jeep and Detroit-driving skills and taking a bus. However, there had been no buses for days, and there probably wasn't a human within 40 miles. "Getting out of here will be an act of God, and I don't dare try it alone," he thought.

They changed seats without leaving the vehicle and sat in silence for a long minute. Ardell said, "Let's pray," and they did pray, audibly and reverently. Ardell started the motor, selected a gear on the manual transmission, and eased out on the clutch for a rearward movement. The

RPM idle speed of the motor was too high to avoid spinning the wheels. That was the last thing he wanted, for when wheels begin to spin out, it is evident that the vehicle isn't going anywhere. A load of despair and a feeling of helplessness came over him. The problem seemed to go from bad to worse. He made a lower gear selection and began to play lightly with the clutch, engaging it gently with very light touches. While being in reverse gear, it felt like there was a movement of the vehicle for a couple of inches. He changed the gear to a forward motion and got the same impression of a tiny move of the jeep. Again he reversed the gear doing the same thing while sensing once more a movement of the jeep. With the inches of forward and rearward movement of the heavily loaded jeep, he began to wear down the high mound of slick, soft earth under the body of the vehicle. With that wear away, the wheels were beginning to gain a little more traction, and the forward and rearward movements became a foot, then more. Not knowing the depth of what lay before them, Ardell chose to back out of their bogged down position. After patiently working forward and rearward movements for several minutes, enough faith and courage seized upon him to make an escape drive rearward. Ardell tried it and found it working so well that he backed up to a vantage point to survey the whole scene. It was a calculated risk, but he chose a different route through the muck, gained some momentum, and slid and bumped through it to become the hero of the wilderness.

Ardell kept driving until they approached Trinidad. It was long after dark. Howard was content to be moving over the road until other vehicles were being met, while nearing a small village, and he thought the glare of auto lights were too troublesome for the older man. Howard again took the driver's seat and finished the trip about 9 p.m., parking the jeep on deserted streets in mid-town Trinidad. The jeep was too muddy to be recognizable as anything more than something with wheels. Surely Rafael had long given up on their arrival at 5 p.m. and had gone to his room for the night.

There was, however, a welcoming party of one lonely woman. She was a beggar asking for money to feed her children. Preoccupied with the whereabouts of Rafael, a room for the night, and making a phone call to their wives back home to announce their arrival, Ardell kept turning from the insistent woman who wanted money. The beggar woman who knew no courtesy or timidity would not take the brush off. Ardell finally told her to bring the children and he would feed them. She put up excuses for not having them with her and could not bring them. Ardell had adopted his own policy for giving to beggars but never giving money. He had bought eyeglasses, dentures, school supplies, medicine, food, clothes, and over the space of a year would spend a few thousand dollars doing this. He chose those that had need and could not help themselves. There were men in the United States back home that had chosen Ardell to distribute their charity funds in this manner, and he tried faithfully to honor their wishes in giving. If anyone was smoking or drinking and known to be separated from family as a non-supporting father or a woman of the street, they never received more than a little food. The truth is that he had become a little callused in this country where begging had become an industry, preying upon tourists as much as possible and everybody in general.

The woman was wearing shoes, looked clean enough, and was adequately dressed. She finally gave up on her quest for money and left. Rafael had not given up on the arrival of his friends and was still walking the area of the city's central plaza looking for his friends or their jeep. The travelers arrived nearly four hours late, but they found one another. As they exchanged jubilant greetings, Ardell asked about the local office of Intel, the phone company in town. "They close at nine o'clock," Rafael said, "and it is here, close by." Off they ran to be the last customers of the day getting their telephone call through. Without having telephone lines in that remote area, calls were made by a short-wave radio system.

A hotel room was found. It had accommodations much like those that cowboys found in Dodge City, Kansas, in the 1870s. Howard and Ardell retired for the night, but weariness of soul and body drove sleep away. Ardell's mind was full of troubling thoughts in the dark and quietness of rustic surroundings in the frontier town. He thought again of the beggar woman whom he spurned on the street, when they arrived earlier in the night. "Would it be possible that she were not what he thought she was, just another opportunist that hit upon the strangers that came to town?" When he remembered the Bible book of Hebrews that says, "Be not forgetful to entertain strangers; for thereby some have entertained angels unawares," other questions came to mind. "Could the strange woman have been an angel unawares, and not just an opportunist?" A third possibility smote his conscience as grievously. "It just may be that she wasn't an angel or an opportunist but truly a woman wanting to provide something to eat for her children. If that be the case," he surmised, "then there is at least one person in this town tonight that knows me as the wealthy foreigner and has become the despicable one of the city." She's probably saying, "He could help, and wouldn't."

He began to drift off to sleep, wanting to be remembered as the hero of the wilderness, but knowing fully well that he will probably be remembered longer as the despicable one of the city. It's not a pleasant thought for one who came so far—to perform good—to become so victimized in conscience.

Epilogue: On Monday, February 3, 1997, Howard and Ardell started the two-day drive back to Cochabamba. After a five-day shut down of bus

Vondas A. Smith

service, buses also began to run again. Out on the road for the second day
of the return trip, they learned that a river bridge had washed away, and the
detour added another day to homeward travel by a different and longer
route.

~~~~~~

View from Phone Booth
Written June 15, 1993

<u>Prologue</u>: In different places and in different manners, strange things seem to happen in the lives of young boys. More often than not, he neither knows how to tell them or to whom it should be told. To this author, the first such incident came out of the dark in a movie theater and was more frightening to him at that time than any horror movie he had ever seen. Again it occurred when he was still a youth, while hitchhiking on a lonely road one night. This time the offender was a high school coach.

    —As age matures a boy into manhood, the frightening aspect of such occurrences evolves to become repulsively abnormal, disdainful, and repugnant. The author once found two Army cooks together in bed locked in arms as lovers as he alerted them to arise to start their day in the kitchen to prepare breakfast for a company of soldiers. He didn't report it hoping that it would somehow miraculously go away. He hoped it wouldn't be found out that he was even acquainted with them.—

The quirks of perversion are many, and even the most traveled and best informed can become astounded at things he sees and hears. What is recorded here happened in the adult life of the boy who fought off a man's hands in the dark theater nearly 40 years earlier in life. Personal diary notes indicate this to have happened in the vicinity of 300 W. 92nd Street in New York in July 1980.

Arriving early for an evening appointment at a church meeting, a man and his wife had parked their vehicle and decided to stroll around on the streets some. There were still a few hours of the afternoon left to them, and a sandwich and soft drink appealed to their appetites, especially if they could find a nice air-conditioned place to enjoy it. They were leisurely enjoying a stroll in the new surroundings. They were in New York, the big city, which sometimes is adoringly referred to as the "Big Apple."

The pedestrians moving about on that afternoon did not appear to be whiling away their time, and there were numbers of vehicles which made the streets relatively busy. All the street activity caused the newly arrived couple to feel a little estranged from their surroundings; however, they were in no way uncomfortable.

While exchanging small talk, they made an occasional pause to take a long look at the street name, especially if they were about to cross a street. Sooner or later they would want to return to their car. Once—when about to cross an intersection—the newly arrived strangers in the big city glanced to the right at a party of five or six walking together at a relatively quick pace. The well-dressed party silently passed immediately in front of the strolling couple.

At least three of the curious party were women who led the way walking briskly. The high heels that the women wore caused them to surpass the height to be called petite. They wore their cosmetics heavily, but professionally, applied. With skill, their hair was styled becomingly and was pleasantly long. The dresses were not the quality that one might expect to find in a dollar store. Money and good taste had secured for them some of the finest in dress, and they were apparently on their way to a social function.

As the visiting couple looked on curiously, the husband became petrified with indescribable awe, trying to connect the feminine factors of the women with those that would cause him to want to whistle, if he were younger and back in his small home town. It isn't known if the husband even made a sound, but his perplexed gaze caused his wife to become nervously uncomfortable. She became sufficiently unfixed to physically shove him toward a phone booth close by. Before losing his hypnotic-like trance, she forced him into the phone booth and kept the door secure until the scene passed on.

Just surely as birds know birds, women know women. As the husband looked on from the street side phone booth from where the wife hoped he would feign to make a call, his perception began to awaken. Why were their feet so large and their legs muscular enough for a world-cup class soccer champion? To be young women, they were conspicuously out of balance to be the lovely proportioned ones in hips and waist. Though beautiful women may sometimes have broad shoulders, and some even enhance that look with padded clothing, those ladies' shoulders could have brought them a union card in a stevedore union lodge in any port.

The ladies walked on out of sight, and the two or three big men that accompanied them followed close behind. The men were obviously guards and carried a stance of being fearless and well disciplined. These relationships began to speak for themselves after the spectacle had passed.

As the wide-eyed and speechless husband emerged from the phone booth, his facial expression asked a silent question, and his wife had a ready answer. She angrily snapped, "Those were all men, you dummy."

~~~~~~~~~~~~~~~~~~~~~~~~~~~~~~~~~~~~~

Vondas A. Smith

We Call It That in Wisconsin

Written November 27, 1989

During 1971, most folks thought that tourism would be good and safe in the Mideastern part of the world. It was then that a homebody ventured out. He had never been off the continent of North America and wanted to see the Holy Land, which he did, in the course of that trip.

There were 22 in the package tour group that the new traveler joined. The host of the group was named Thomas. He had done well to keep expenses down, as well as scheduling several countries including some of Europe. The new traveler's wife and children accompanied him as far as the plane to see his departure. During those emotional moments, the traveler forgot to hand over the keys to the car parked out on the airport parking lot. He never realized his mistake until he arrived in London. About to retire for his first night abroad, he emptied the contents of his pocket and was stunned to find the car keys still with him. "What did my wife and children do, and how did they get home?" he wondered.

The traveling husband and father, one of the group of 22, was assigned to share hotel rooms with another man traveling single. His name was Steve. They became well acquainted because of their close association. They kept notes, made pictures, were prompt for the start of their guided daily tours, and would go out strolling together during their free time.

It was on Sunday afternoon, the second of their three-day visit to London that the traveling father and Steve were out on their own in the London streets near the hotel. It was a beautiful afternoon in London as the two strolled out to view the neighborhood about the hotel where they were staying. Being the day that it was, there were no shops open. Indeed the two men weren't out looking for anything to buy anyway. They were just two curious sight seekers, out on the vacated streets, peering into store windows.

A woman came into view that was obviously doing some self-entertaining with the occupation of leisure. She did not purposefully approach the two men nor did they seek conversation with her. The three did find themselves looking into the windows of the same store, however, in their passing by. One of those men, he that carried his car keys to Europe, at least decided that he would be civil and speak.

In his awkward way and unable to think of anything meaningful to say, he broke the silence. With a smile he acknowledged her presence and said, "We call this window shopping back in Tennessee, in the United States." "Yes," she said, "That's what we call it in Wisconsin, too." "Small world," he thought. "I'm not so far from home after all."

~~~~~~~~~~~~~~~~~~~~~~~~~~~~~~~~~~~~~

Dining Hall Shoot Out

Written November 17, 1989

Prologue: The Biblical patriarch, Jacob, deceived his father, Isaac, only to fall victim to deception by his father-in-law, Laban. It's sweet to be on the winning end, but one can question the value of winning if it brings another conflict resulting in a loss.

Ernest tells the story that involved himself and a friend named Claiborn. The two of them had been classmates in a seminary some years before, and their friendship was long standing. Here is a frightening episode of one encounter together that took place during a summer church camp.

Either of the two could rightly be called a prankster. Claiborn was especially fond of impersonating another, and strangely enough, it was only for his own fun. None were able to charge him with doing anything wrong, but he did move a few hearts to hand out some small offerings of money or food.

It began to happen at night. After the church camp activities of the day, Claiborn would dress as an old woman. His clothing, his posture, and his voice were all so near perfect that he was able to disguise his real identity even from those that knew him. There were lots of individual cabins on the spacious grounds of the church camp. Most of these were individually owned and were designated by the name of the owner. Many, but not all of them, were cabins belonging to ministers.

There were lots of laughs and fun on the side for Claiborn, but others were wondering about that pitiful old woman. How was she coming on the camp at such a late hour at night to beg? Claiborn, as if he were a she, would go from door-to-door begging for presumed grandchildren or under some other pretext. He was getting a few "hand outs," but most of all he was getting lots of sympathy.

The identity of that sad "old woman" was most troubling. His prankster fun was doing well until another prankster became interested. This was where Ernest came in. It isn't remembered at this late date how Ernest became aware of the real identity of the "old beggar woman." He did become aware of the woman's identity, though, and then he set about to turn the table and have some fun of his own. Ernest had to solicit the help of other trusted men to assist him. They planned their strategy.

Claiborn was a good pianist, and in the camp dining hall there was a piano. It occupied one corner of the huge dining area, and Claiborn enjoyed playing there in the early afternoon after lunch. It was in such a setting, and at such a time of the day, that these few men decided that Claiborn must pay for his fun.

The dining area was occupied by only a few at the chosen time. All were well informed and were in agreement to work the plan. Claiborn was in the corner of the dining area on the piano. He was playing some favorite hymn with ease and enjoying himself. Zero hour arrived, and suddenly Ernest entered. He was a maniac, completely without rationality. Another was pleading with him, trying to reason and restrain him from killing. The target he sought seemed to be anyone that was in shooting range. In his hand was his pistol, and it was being waved wildly as he screamed threats to anyone and everyone that stood against him. He charged that his friends had become traitors and besmirched his name and ruined his good reputation. His wild and insane behavior threw the whole company into stunned shock.

Ernest's eyes fell on Fred, and with his pistol pointed at him, Ernest screamed why Fred was to be the first to die. Two blasts from his pistol, and Fred screamed out, begging, as he fell across a table. The piano music was silenced in the corner, and fearful eyes from the man on the piano bench beheld the whole scene in horror. Fred rolled from the table and fell to the floor in his ketchup blood.

Fred was writhing in the throes of death, as he fell from the table to the floor with the red-like ketchup blood spilling everywhere. Another man began to flee and was shot while he fled, knocking him screaming to the floor. A third man was slain by a single bullet. These were long-time friends to Ernest but they had, as Ernest was screaming out, become character assassinators and ruined him. At that time, the eye of the pistol marksman fell upon Claiborn who was half standing and cowering in the corner. Ernest screamed out to Claiborn, "I know what you've been telling everyone against me, and you'll pay for that with your blood." Claiborn came alive with all the pleading and crying that could burst from a man in anguish. He begged Ernest to spare his life. Ernest paused for the briefest five seconds as if to take careful aim and all the while the crescendo of lamentation from Claiborn reached far beyond the confines of the dining hall. Appearing to be a crazy man, Ernest posed a smirkey smile, as he was about to kill Claiborn with a single shot. At least three lay silent and still on the floor, and Claiborn was cornered and about to die at the hand of the smirkey man with the smoking pistol. Ernest fired off a well-aimed single shot amid screams from Claiborn, "In the name of God, no, no, no!"

There were no deaths from pistol wounds since it was only loaded with blank cartridges. Claiborn's momentary heart failure gradually began to recover as the presumably slain began to get up from the floor. There were giggles from all but Claiborn as they saw him search for blood and wounds that weren't there.

It isn't known what Claiborn did with his beggar woman attire. What is known, though, is that the campground church folks ceased to be troubled with a poor begging woman that kept such late hours.

~~~~~~~~~~~~~~~~~~~~~~~~~~~~~~~

Careful, He's for Real

Written September 26, 1989, La Paz, Bolivia

While doing some preparatory stateside work for promotion before departing for an overseas assignment, Sadnov and his wife had an appointment with a church pastor in a state west of the Mississippi River. Meeting new people wasn't a dread for the couple, but they endeavored to find common ground for conversation about things they mutually enjoyed. With the first sight and handshake, the two preachers were immediate friends. The host pastor was a woodsman, it was later learned, and he was still active in the sawmill business. With complete ease and enjoyment, the two men discovered that they spoke the same language.

Literally, their conversation was spiced with "younses, plumb nearly, purit nu'art, down yonder, right smart, tolably well, much obliged, and notin past a'common," etc. Sadnov was having a holiday, thinking perhaps he had found some of his dad's lost relatives. After all, his granddad was born in St. Joseph, Missouri, back in 1874. Both men used their extracurricular vocabulary with such ease that Sadnov's wife became content to just listen. There was another factor, however, to be taken into consideration in this whole new acquaintance. After all, the host pastor had a family. The two wives began their own conversational exchange, and it was accompanied with the sincerest of all courtesies.

Shortly thereafter, Sadnov was made aware that his wife would like to have his help at something. She had feigned her need in order to summons him apart for a brief word of wifely council. In the most direct admonition from a caring wife, Sadnov heard the conclusion to this matter according to a woman's wisdom. He quickly heard from her that for him to do anything less than to give heed would be catastrophic. Being startled by the wife's revelation, Sadnov's "country jargon" began to take on a language sound that was a little more contemporary, at least to him.

"Dear, these good folks are for real," she advised. "You're putting on with your part of your grandparents' language, but this family talks like that." "If you keep on, you're going to slip up, and they'll think you're making fun of them."

Vondas A. Smith

A Lovely Bunch of Beauties

Written October 14, 1989, La Paz, Bolivia

Prologue: *Learning comes in portions because there are fractional degrees of the assimilation of information. The full story isn't always apparent at the present, and this once happened to a traveler on the U.S./Mexican border.*

By invitation from a Mexican youth studying in the United States, two unmarried seminarians accompanied him on a tour of Mexico one summer. The Mexican youth, a minister, had many acquaintances in his native country, and the boys' travel costs were minimal. One of the U.S. citizens had about $30 when they crossed the border into Mexico at El Paso during the last days of May. The same youth named Sadnov received $10 in the mail from his mother during a two-week stay in Mexico City.

Since their expenses were all paid, money wasn't necessarily important except for the need to purchase a small gift. It was their health in the hot summer of Mexico that was troubling. One of the English-speaking youths fell ill in Southwest Mexico, and he was forced to cut his visit short and return to Albuquerque, New Mexico. Sadnov didn't escape losing the key, a term in Mexican slang meaning that he had diarrhea. He was tough, but he slowly lost weight for six weeks. He desperately tried to be a Mexican, but it wasn't working well.

On one Monday morning in July, they were about 70 miles from anywhere in a remote mountain village. Sadnov and his guide awaited the mail hack and contracted passage with the mailman back to the city where there was a railroad. Directional travel was northward toward the U.S. border, which was about 500 miles away from the starting point.

For reason of route and prearranged appointments, Sadnov's interpreter guide had to leave the train during their northward travel. This left the English-speaking traveler alone. He found himself needing another $10 bill from his mother to go with what he had. Nogales, Arizona, was the last stop of the train travel, but from there he could resort to U.S. highways and travel by thumb, hitchhiking.

Arriving in Nogales, there was one luxury the sick youth needed to afford himself with his last cash. He had been on the train a day and a night with no rest and little to eat. He got off the train on the Mexican side of the border with suitcase in hand and began to hunt an economy meal and the cheapest bed in town. He found both, and he still had $5 left out of his $10 bill.

The hotel room cost him $3 and was just a place with a pillow to rest his head. It did not have air-conditioning, and the July night heat on the border made him restless. Though he was sick, tired, and restless, he continued to be driven outside for some air well into the night.

Now for the purpose of speaking English again, there were plenty of people around him that night, and they appeared to have leisure time on hand. They all seemed to move about as singles, and yet the hall of the hotel was full. The atmosphere was pleasant enough, but there was something strange about it all.

Things didn't seem to fit together properly on that night in Nogales, in the border town's hotel. Some years later, however, after traveling more and becoming much wiser, Sadnov began to see the picture more clearly. The reason for the dozen or more beautiful young girls, which continuously paraded alone in the hotel that night, was to find a lonely traveler that spoke their native language.

The next morning the young seminarian began to catch rides on the blistering hot July day in Arizona, leaving the Mexican border farther to the south. There were two things that occupied most of his thoughts. "How can I stretch my $5 for a couple more days, and why were there so many lovely girls in that hotel last night?"

~~~~~~~~~~~~~~~~~~~~~~~~~~~~~~~~~~

About the Author

Vondas A. Smith is a minister, church founder, and retired foreign missionary. He is a theology graduate of the former Pentecostal Bible Institute, Tupelo, Mississippi. After his graduation in 1950, Rev. Smith founded the United Pentecostal Church of Newport, Arkansas, and served as editor of the *Arkansas Messenger*, the church's state publication. In 1963, Vondas Smith founded the Whitehaven United Pentecostal Church of Memphis, Tennessee, presently known as The Pentecostal Church of Memphis. He served 24 years as a foreign missionary to Bolivia, South America, from September 1973 through August 1997. While working in Bolivia, Rev. Smith established churches in five of the nation's nine departments (states). He also founded Bolivia's Bible Institute, the Instituto de Doctrina Apostolica, in Cochabamba, Bolivia. In 1996, Rev. Smith founded a religious book translation/publishing entity called Rabi Publicaciones in La Paz, Bolivia, and he is presently directing this endeavor from retirement. After his retirement and return to Tennessee, Rev. Smith assumed the directorship of both the English- and Spanish-speaking prison ministries of The Pentecostal Church in October 1998. He recently resigned from the English language ministry to focus his energy into founding a Spanish-speaking ministry at The Pentecostal Church of Memphis. This new ministry began in May 1999. Rev. Smith has been married to the former Leah Ruth Ellis since 1948, and they have five children, 14 grandchildren, and two great-grandchildren.

Printed in the United States
857400003B